THE INVESTIGATOR

THE INVESTIGATOR

BY

RICHARD MOORE

STORY LINE PRESS

1991

Copyright ©1991 by Richard Moore

First American Printing

All rights reserved. No part of this book may be reproduced in any form or by any electronic or mechanical means including information storage and retrieval systems without permission in writing from the publisher, except by a reviewer.

ISBN: 0-934257-77-9

Published by Story Line Press
Three Oaks Farm
Brownsville, OR
97327-9718

The author is grateful to the Djerassi Foundation, where some of the work on this novel took place.

Excerpts from this novel have appeared in *Negative Capability* and *The Portland Review of the Arts*

In memory of Basil Chadwick

ONE

He lived in a large brick house in an expensive suburb with his older brother and sister, and the neighbors suspected, though they could not be sure, that he was mad. Not raving mad. Not dangerous—though who could ever be sure about that? But at the very least, breathtakingly peculiar. The improbable menage suggested it. In that huge house set back from the road amidst towering, exquisitely cared-for cypresses, copper beeches and maples on a full acre of green-golden lawn and gardens a short walk from Sweethill Center, just the three of them, two unmarried brothers and a sister: Edward, the eldest, already emerging on the doddering side of middle age, Clara showing streaks of gray and growing husky-voiced, and him, Archibald, once so darkly handsome, heavier now, and portly, the one for whom all three seemed to exist. It was unnatural. Edward and Clara worked and were out all day, Edward an executive for an ice cream company, Clara with a real estate firm in the city: but Archibald was always there, mowing the lawn in summer, shoveling snow in winter, putting up their old-fashioned wooden storm windows in the fall, taking them down in the spring, and in all seasons going in and out on mysterious little errands in his bright orange Volkswagen bug.

Edward and Clara had cars of their own, American cars, Edward a small green Mercury, Clara a large green Cadillac. There was plenty of money evidently, inherited from Edward Bromley, Sr., the neurosurgeon, who had built the house in the twenties, and they really didn't have to work at all—not for the money. But in Sweethill it is normal to have a job, abnormal not to.

Archibald seemed a perfect illustration of the evils of not working. Year after year in his idleness he spoke less, growing visibly uncomfortable when he had to talk with neighbors, hence gradually not talking at all, keeping his distance, and at last hardly even waving to them from afar. He had grown sloppier over the years too. His old work pants clung baggily to his hips and threatened to fall down completely as he pushed their old mower over the vast lawn. The mower sputtered and misfired. How did he ever get it started with the engine so badly out of tune? PUTT, PUTT, PUTT, PUTTER, PUTT, it went with Archibald lumbering after it in and out of his arboreal glooms. "I do it for the exercise," he had explained laconically years ago when he still spoke to the neighbors. And now just last week, a housewife who lived across the street said to her husband, "Henry, you know that Archibald Bromley whose pants always look as though they are going to fall down? Well, this afternoon I saw him. He was out on his lawn, squatting and digging up dandelions, and his pants had come down so far that his bare white cheeks were right there, completely exposed. It was obscene."

"And were you excited by the sight?" Henry asked with more sarcasm than he had intended. And with this error another nasty evening had begun at the Melbys.

In fact, Nora Melby was a little obsessed on the subject of the Bromleys. "That Clara has quite a cosy little life for herself with her two devoted males in constant attendance. There I am in the winter after every snowstorm, shoveling out our little driveway, and there he is, big burly Archibald, clearing off the windshield of her Cadillac with the engine running. Then out she comes, all bright and neat and faultlessly dressed and steps into her nice warm car and drives away.

"Really amazing she is. Hair always perfectly set, never a strand out of place. Never a shabby stitch on her anywhere. Always wearing the same shiny pumps—black ones in winter, white ones, just as clean and shiny, in the summer. Always perfectly made up. What's she like inside the house I wonder? I'll bet she's perfectly made up the moment she steps out of her bedroom in the morning. I wonder if either one of her brothers (I suppose they *are* her brothers) has ever had the shock of seeing her without her make-up, no eyebrows or lips, dead white face, hair in an old gray hairnet, so she won't get it disturbed in the night."

"For God's sake, Nora, shut up! She's a very handsome woman."

Many people had seen what Nora had seen. In the supermarket Clara and Edward like an old married couple, slowly growing out of date, she in her impeccable robin's-egg blue coat, he in his eternal gray suit with a vest and gold watch chain, wearing a straw Panama hat or a trilby, depending on the season, pushing the cart for her, while she put things into it. The same things? Yes, surely, always the same things.

As a rule, people in Sweethill didn't mind strange menages. There were few uneasy feelings about the little flagstone house on Cornell Avenue occupied by the paunchy uncertain-looking young man with a loose pimpled face and long flaxen hair, who had a different car in his driveway every week and a different boy on his lawn, working the electric lawn mower. Every night till the early morning the light seeped behind the drawn blinds. They didn't mind that. That was new and modern. But the strangeness of the Bromleys was from the past, where their own roots were.

There were two aspects of Sweethill. On the one hand it was a desirable suburb of a large city and was merely a part of that city—a carefully cleansed and manicured part—and on the other it was an independent small town planted in its own traditions and reaching into its own past. So in the quiet streets that crisscrossed its high ground and in the houses they linked together, relentlessly increasing in value with the years, there were the old residents who could remember their youth in Sweethill's lanes, playgrounds and schools, and there were the newcomers, the ones with bright futures who kept the real estate market healthy and whose memories lay elsewhere. The Bromleys qualified as old residents. Their house had stood for a full generation now, and Archibald had been born in it. Unlike Edward and Clara, he was remembered by everyone, especially the girls, as someone altogether apart, wild, wonderful, with his quick, lithe body and the dark hair falling in great waves over his gray-green eyes. In his first two years at the local highschool he was already beginning to make a name for himself in basketball and track, and Gladys Worthington, for one, now a middle-aged spinster, still living two streets away, had never quite forgiven Archibald's father for sending him to a boarding school in Connecticut for the next two years. And there was a retired mathematics teacher, too, living in Sweethill, who still regretted losing to that boarding school the best, the most extraordinary student she ever had.

But there was something unpleasant and frightening about him too. He played the same games as others but with a single-mindedness sometimes and a logical intensity that seemed to obliterate their reality as games. One season, for example, in a curious emergence of Freudian symbolism, it became all the rage for boys to squirt girls with waterpistols. The fad would have come and gone harmlessly and been long forgotten, if Archibald had not thought one day of filling his waterpistol with ink....

Then there were the fireworks on Halloween. Each year on that evening, along with the odd daubings of paint and smears of soap where they were prominent but not destructive, there were desultory explosions of firecrackers saved from the previous Fourth of July. But on this particular Halloween there was a new sound. A week before, Archibald had gone to a plumbing supply house and bought several pieces of iron pipe, each three inches long and threaded on both ends, and he also asked for iron caps to fit the ends. The plumber was suspicious but could not have said of what and did not know that the boy had accumulated a sizable hoard of gunpowder in an old cocoa can. (The Bromleys were members of a yacht club, where a little cannon was used to salute the raising and lowering of the flag, and the supply of cartridges for it was poorly guarded.)

Archibald capped the pipes at one end, filled them with the black, acrid-smelling powder, then screwed on the second cap, in which he had drilled a small hole for an old fire-cracker fuse. The result was a bomb powerful enough to wake the town and panic the police department. It was evidently one of these that blew a loose stone from the foundation of Snelling's Candy Store and another that crippled the lamppost in Sweetblossom Lane. The spirit of Halloween, in which the demons were allowed to mock for an evening all that was good and sacred, had plainly gone too far.

The next day garrulous Archie told his friends how he had been going home late with one of the pipe bombs still in his pocket when a police car pulled up beside him and the officer asked him if he had heard the explosions. "There's some nut around who's setting off handgrenades or mortar shells."

There was the same apparent recklessness in his telling about it as there had been in the exploit itself—and the same fine sense of calculation. If the police heard his tales, what could they do? There was no acceptable proof in what might, after all, have been only empty bragging. And more important, what would they want to do? Knowing that the prankster was Archibald Bromley, the son of Doctor Bromley, and not some fugitive from a prison or asylum, would be reassuring; and to have pressed charges against the family of such a prominent taxpayer would have seemed petty.

But were the police and others really as helpless as the boy imagined? Or could it have been this incident and others like it (the flame thrower; the toy cannon that was no toy) that prompted Doctor Bromley to send him to the Queensbury School for Boys the following autumn? That was the same school, on its island in the Connecticut River, that Edward had attended ten years before. The tradition of sending the sons of Bromley for their final two years of highschool before matriculating at Harvard had already been established. But Edward had been a mediocre student. Edward needed Queensbury's more intense academic discipline. What was it that Archibald needed? His father said he needed the closeness to his own kind that he would come to feel in a dormitory: he needed a deeper appreciation of how society was founded on a sense of moderation and on certain codes of behavior that ought not be questioned.

But something went very wrong at Queensbury. When

he had finished his two years there, he was not, to his father's consternation, ready for Harvard, but for training as a paratrooper. And when he returned from the paratroops two years after that, he was only fit evidently to become what in the following twenty-four years he became. There was hardly anyone who had known Archibald from the beginning who did not wonder with some degree of bewilderment and pain how he came to be the way he was and what further harm still might come of it.

TWO

"Time to get up, Archie!"

He had already been awakened by the Melby's dog, whose bark, he sometimes thought, could penetrate death itself, and he lay there, thinking about chucking it for the day. He had done that once or twice as a new thing this past year: just not gotten up at all. Lay there daydreaming the whole day. Clara seemed to think it was some kind of scandal, but what harm did it do? What difference did it make? She could have done the same thing, and that, he decided, was what made her furious: being reminded by his actions how unnecessary to anyone her own life was. What astonished him was how exhausted he had been when his usual bedtime came round—as though he had spent the day hiking in the mountains. Maybe he had. His own mountains. Wasn't there something going on today that he wanted to avoid at all costs? He couldn't remember what.

"Archie?"

"Right. On my way." Clara always called him from the doorway across the landing, never venturing into his part of the house. In recent years her voice had been getting a bit husky and gravelly (the effect of booze on middle-aged women) and when she tried to force it back up into a girlish high pitch, he thought nastily, she only made it sound like the yipping of Nora Melby's dog. Why did she always have to put on that phony exterior, that pretense of girlish innocence?

When he arrived in the kitchen, Edward was at the table dressed in his business suit with the golden watch chain dangling. He was sipping coffee and reading the paper, but looked up.

"Morning, Arch."

Just coffee. Nothing more. Amazing how little he ate.

"You really ought to have something to eat for breakfast, Ed dear," said Clara, standing by the counter, "You're beginning to look awfully run-down." She had clear, almost sharp features, and Archibald, who had been struck by the way her words echoed his thought, found himself admiring the elegance of her profile as she watched the toaster and swept some crumbs onto a plate with a folded napkin. Her eyes were brown, her eyebrows plucked and dark, and her hair still had hints of its youthful blondness. She wore a pink frilly apron over her business dress, and a little white bunny embroidered on the top part of the apron went nicely with her pumps: made them seem like little white bunnies too, hopping beneath her as she walked about the kitchen. Ridiculous the way she dressed!

"Are you going to the funeral today, Archie?"

"Funeral?" He was getting his glass of gingerale from the refrigerator.

"Don't tell me you've forgotten, dear! Priscilla

Cameron, your old mathematics teacher. You know, the one who thought you were such a genius. She'd be glad to know you came to say goodbye."

"She won't know whether I came or not."

"Archie!"

"O. K. I'll think about it."

"If you think about it, you won't go. I'm sure your old flame, Gladys Worthington, is going to be there."

"Get off that, Clara!"

"Go on. I know you've always had a soft spot in your heart for Gladys. And I'm certain she adores you. Always has, always will."

"Clara, look, you know I don't have anything to say to people like that any more, so why do you torment me?"

"I didn't mean to torment you, Archie. We only want to help you. Help you get out and enjoy yourself. Enjoy living. Edward, dear, tell Archie that's what we want. Tell him we love him and have always wanted the best for him."

Edward looked up and smiled mildly. There was something absurd about his florid, emaciated face with its bulbous nose and narrow bristly moustache; but his eyes glittered darkly and were beautiful—like a cow's eyes, full of a melancholy tenderness. "Yes, Clara, my dear, of course we want the best for him."

"Dear, dear, my dear," said Archibald. "I'm going to leave you two love birds alone with each other and go back to bed."

He left his gingerale glass drained on the table and headed for the back stairs with only an astonished yip from Clara following him. Edward, he knew, was stunned. They both hated his taunts about them being lovers or being married, were indeed very sensitive on the subject, so it made a good weapon.

He actually did get back into bed. There was still a little drowsiness in him that he could summon, even after the excitement below, and he loved to close his eyes and contemplate the uncertain fleeting images that hovered between sleep and waking. It delighted him how deftly and easily in that state his body seemed to slip into and out of its existence between the sheets.

He was sinking inward, had been for years. Sometimes as the wakefulness grew and the events of his outward life again became a presence in his reverie, he thought pleasantly about old triumphs, things he had invented and mathematical problems he had solved. And sometimes those thoughts led him, less pleasantly, to examine the process by which a person of talent and promise had been transformed into the useless thing lying there.

He thought it might be pleasant this morning and, of course, appropriate, to play host to his memories of Priscilla Cameron: maybe relive an incident or two in her class. His conquest of her tetrahedrons maybe.... But his mind seemed to grow vague and lackadaisical in that quarter, and he had to admit finally that he really wasn't much interested any more in Priscilla Cameron and her tetrahedrons.

"Quit smirking at me, O'Connell!"

He contemplated the image of a fifteen year old boy, pale, arrogant, heavy-lidded, stirring in the shadows of the Queensbury Academy. "Why did I ever become friends with someone as sly and stupid as you?"

"Look who's talking. Look who's lying there," said the image.

"You were some kind of brilliant success, then, O'Connell?"

"Moderate, Bromley. Moderate. A fair-sized insurance agency."

"You weren't good at anything. Not any sport. Not any subject."

"You admired my wit, Bromley, my charm. You needed me to keep in touch. But it was *me*, you know, who used *you*. You never realized that? I'd never have made it through second year algebra without you."

Archibald sighed. Queensbury had bewildered and depressed him; but the mathematics had kept coming and coming, storming him with ideas, like an impersonal force, virtually making him its instrument...

"God's little ukulele," said O'Connell, "...until he had gone far beyond all his courses and all the books on the subject in the school library. Was it a pity that he didn't have better teachers?"

"You know, O'Connell, that first summer I got really involved with permutations and combinations.... You know..."

"No I don't know, and don't tell me."

"...and just about rediscovered group theory for myself. I didn't even realize it or find out what group theory was until after I got out of the Army, browsing in the library here in Sweethill."

"O bully, bully for Bromley!"

"Yes, bully. I hardly even understood it any more, when I found it in the book... O'Connell... what went wrong?"

"None of us knew what to make of you. But cripes, Bromley, you did alright. Top scorer in basketball our junior year. But then the next year why did you have to spoil everything and decide you didn't like the game any more and didn't want to play? And them trying to make you, until that game with Sandbottom, when you missed every shot. You couldn't have made it more obvious. I don't think old Wintergreen ever forgave you. Can you blame him? Can you really blame him, Bromley? What else did the old fart have but that school? And you were telling him to take his school and its athletic honor and shove it. I never really understood why you did that."

"Athletics are supposed to be a joy, not a business."

"Bullshit. Everything's a business. You mean you still haven't learned that after all these years?"

Archibald lifted his top sheet with his thumbs and forefingers, then raised his knees, drawing fresh air in around his body.

"Other people did things much worse than you did," O'Connell continued. "I mean like—the fairies in that place. I don't think you had any idea. But the things you did were all so...they were harmless, they were even silly, but they were all so strange—I mean, really unheard of. Your nightlight, drilling into Forest's wall for his all night electricity. That illegal weekend you took, just walking off, thinking no one would notice you were gone, and they almost didn't. But I guess it was your nightlight finally...."

Archibald felt a growing impatience. "*Our* nightlights, you dumb Harp. I had the idea and did it perfectly—my best practical invention ever. But then you had to try the same thing, not because you had anything you wanted to read. You've never read a book in your life."

"I have too read a book...."

"I told you it wouldn't work, going into that corridor light switch, filling up your whole closet with plaster, looking for it. What a mess. And then when you turned on your light, the corridor lights came on halfway."

"You didn't know that would happen any more than I did."

"How could old Nelly Forest help but discover you? And he realized right away you were too dumb to think up anything like that. Things like that came from me. So he opens my door without any evidence, just on that bare suspicion. And there I am in the Galaxy of Andromeda, and there he is, Nelly, The Beak, right in there with me. 'Well, Archibald, this is something—I think you will agree—that Mr. W. will have to hear about.' Nathan Gormley Wintergreen...."

"Our beloved Headmaster."

"No. More than that, O'Connell. The quintessence, the very identity of the Queensbury School. Have you ever heard of the great modern philosopher, Martin Heidegger? No, of course you haven't. According to a nutty little book of his in the Sweethill Library, words in every language but Ancient Greek stand for the things they name, but in that one language, Ancient Greek, they actually *are* the things. That's the way it was with old Nate Gormley. He didn't just stand for the Queensbury Academy, he *was* the Queensbury Academy—down to the last roll of dust in each gloomy classroom, the odor in each warm jockstrap, the torn pages in every tattered textbook. Individuals didn't exist for him. Even when he was two feet away from you, he used the same voice he used, addressing the whole school. You could imagine him raping somebody...."

"Man, woman, or beast."

"But talking intimately with a woman by candlelight...."

"Never!"

"I had to see him about my light, O'Connell. You did too, about yours. But you he could forgive."

"I played on the teams. I never tried going on an illegal weekend."

"My aunt covered for me. Wrote a letter from New York. My terminally ill grandmother had taken a turn for the worse."

"Your grandmother was a whore in the Bronx, and she took a turn for twenty dollars. Gravely gave you her address."

"When he stood there in the dining hall with that letter half crumpled in his hairy fist and his eyebrows twitching and his voice choking in fury, you know, O'Connell, I wanted to laugh. And he could see that I wanted to laugh."

Gloom came over Archibald's face as he pulled the covers up around his beard stubble and waited for yet another yip from Nora Melby's dog, Hannibal, who had evidently been let out for a second time that morning. The truly excruciating thing about a dog barking, what made its effect on the nerves so devastating, he decided, was its irregularity. You never knew when the next piercing sound was going to come, and so there was no way to prepare for it and build it into the background of your awareness.

Mr. W. sat in his office, a gray forelock dipping over the great box of his face, when Forest led Archibald into his presence the day after discovering the nightlights. The Headmaster was not visibly angry, seemed only saddened and philosophical. He had accepted Archibald in his school without question, he said, because he respected Dr. Bromley's great gifts and reputation as a surgeon and because Archibald's elder brother, Edwin, had been such a fine, such a well-behaved and cooperative boy many years before. But he had reason to be disappointed and to regret his rashness in accepting Archibald—his too easy trust.

He laid down the pencil he had been holding in the fingers of both hands, and as it lay on the large blue blotter that covered the central part of his desk, that looked to Archibald as though it might have been shipped to Mr. W's office directly from the palace of Queen Victoria. He straightened up in his chair. Since graduation was so near, he would not take disciplinary action, but he would have to reconsider his judgment of Archibald's motivation and talents. He understood that Archibald had applied for Harvard. He should forget that ambition. He should lower his sights. He was not Harvard material.

"O'Connell, what was your interview with him like?"

"Terrifying. Not like yours at all. You know, I frighten pretty easily, always have, and he waved his tusks, stamped his feet, and trumpeted to the ceiling, and I was so frozen with terror, I practically had to be carried out on a stretcher."

"But college...? Where did he? ...You?"

"Bromley, you ignorant pig's asshole. You never heard? I graduated from Yale."

THREE

Archibald decided to get up, shave, and treat himself to the luxury of a substantial breakfast alone in the kitchen. He was not Harvard material and he would not go to Priscilla Cameron's funeral either. One went to funerals to please the living, not the dead, and what person living did he care to please?

Queensbury wasn't to blame. There was nothing there that he couldn't have survived. What then? Where then?

His father, with less than a year before his fatal heart attack, had been devastated by the Harvard verdict. He was a scientist and had to dismiss many of the notions that entered his head as irrational nonsense, but the idea haunted him that he had somehow been to blame for his young wife's cancer five years before and that the bad news Archibald kept generating was his punishment.

That summer there were unpleasant scenes—with the mother gone, who might have clouded issues, created diversions, and otherwise disarmed and mitigated the conflict between the father and son. Positions casually taken, sometimes merely for the turn of a phrase, became fixed and crucial, scenes of battle, consecrated by anguish. What, asked Archibald carelessly, was so special about Harvard? Was he trying to infuriate his father, who was an alumnus? Dr. Bromley took the bait. Since Archibald held a Harvard education in such small esteem, he felt the same, no doubt, about college education in general and probably had no desire to go to college at all. That was quite correct, said Archibald. In that case, said the father, the expense would be saved of putting another son through college...and what sort of work did he plan to do instead? Hell, said Archibald, he had always wondered what it would be like to jump out of an airplane. So he planned to enlist in the army and volunteer for the paratroops.

Those were unsettled times. Edward had been with the Navy in the Pacific Theater for two years and would never see his father again. Clara was 19, with a weird, wild beauty about her but shy and unsure of herself, and in the deteriorating situation she missed Edward terribly. Dr. Bromley could not at first take the paratroops seriously, and for a short while the three of them discussed a small college in Ohio said to have a strong mathematics department. But the conversation could not seem to stay focused on this. Mr. W. kept coming up, and, "Archie," Clara would say, "why do you have to be so unreasonable about him? He must have *some* intelligence, *some* integrity to be the headmaster of a school. You don't even seem bitter. You just seem to want to provoke Dad. And poor Dad ends up defending him against you and defending his opinions about you. Stop doing this to us, Archie."

She began going out with her friends less and less, staying shut up in her room on the third floor. She was there and wouldn't come down when Archibald stood in the front hall with a small suitcase packed, waiting for a friend to drive him to the railroad station and jump school in Fort Bragg, North Carolina.

Archibald watched the cinnamon and sugar dissolve in a puddle of melted butter on hot toast. What was it with him and Clara? He had given her a bad time, perhaps, when he got out of the army. Could he help it if the world was a nastier place than she wanted to pretend it was? He had been shocked at the change in her. She had plucked the thick eyebrows which had made her so striking and found some way to make her lips thinner—seemed to have done everything to suppress her natural color, warmth and sensuousness and, dressing herself in flowery blouses and glossy pumps, to present instead the image of the hardened spinster.

He sipped his coffee. It had reached just the right state: had cooled slightly, and its taste, combining with the sugar, had mellowed. In a moment it would no longer be warm enough to excite his palate properly and its taste would have acquired a faint bitterness....

He sipped and stared ahead at the kitchen wall, and the wall became Dick Burlingame, rakish and handsome with his sensitive mouth and merry eyes, splendid in his uniform and the coveted soft boots of the paratrooper. His skin was deeply tanned, and his hat—not his visored hat, but his little "cunt cap" with two peaks and folds along the top—sat on his head at a jaunty angle. He looked off to his right, where Clara had been, and rolled his tongue in his mouth suggestively.

"O, I say, Arch, I don't like your fucking ahmy," he said in a phony British accent, pretending to imitate Archibald's Eastern uppercrust way of talking.

"Tally-Ho, the Fox!" Archibald yelled in the silent kitchen, smiling for the first time that day. Even in the initial confusion and bewilderment on that barracks floor in North Carolina there had been something he loved. A clarity. An honesty. Or was it the unexpected pleasure, not to have a mathematical thought from one end of the month to the other? He felt released into a great emptiness. Drinking deepened and expanded into a way of life and reduced those two years to a blur in his mind, in which only a few fragmentary scenes and disconnected images remained.

How did he know that Burlingame was already the first string quarterback on the football team of a large Midwestern university when he quit after his sophomore year to enlist? "I just had to get a piece of the real action, Arch." All the connections were lost; and there, simply, was Burlingame, graceful, comic, so obviously superior to every other human being imaginable, that the younger man had been overwhelmed by his attentions.

"I say, Arch, may I change your name from Bromley to Barisol and call you Archibald Barisol? I'm sure you remember the story of how Archibald Barisol spelled his name in school. One day the teacher had each student spell his name in the proper way, which was like this. The student stood up and said, 'My name is John Smith. J-O-H-N. There's your *John*. S-M-I-T-H. There's your *Smith*. There's your *John Smith*,' and, 'Thank you, John Smith!' said the young and pretty teacher, 'You may sit down now.' Then Archibald stood up and said, 'My name is Archibald Barisol. A-R-C-H. There's your *Arch*. I. There's your *eye*. There's your *Archeye*. B-A-L. There's your *ball*. There's your *eyeball*. There's your *Archeyeball*. B-A-R. There's your *bare*. There's your *ballbare*. There's your *eyeballbare*. There's your *Archeyeballbare*. A-S. There's your *ass*. There's your *bare ass*. There's your *ball bare ass*. There's your *eyeball bare ass*. There's your *Archeyeball bare ass*. O-L. There's your *'ole*. There's your *ass 'ole*. There's your *bare ass 'ole*. There's your *ball bare ass 'ole*. There's your *eyeball bare ass 'ole*. There's your *Archeyeball bare ass 'ole.*' And the young and pretty teacher said, 'Thank you, Archibald Barisol! You may sit down now.'"

"That really is a pretty inane story, Dick."

"O indeed, yes, Arch; but you love it just the same and remember it with envy after all these years because your tongue isn't quite agile enough to say it properly, limey though you are, and because it's you."

"Me? No, you, Dick. All that's left of you. That bit of silliness."

"You're about to discover, Arch, that my story expresses you, your innermost, meaningful self, old boy, more than you can imagine at the moment."

Burlingame could make prophetic statements like that because he was dead. He came down in a tree in a little too much wind one day and broke his neck.

That must have been when Archibald's drinking began in earnest—and continued, indeed, more than a full decade into civilian life. But drink and bereavement and the loss of his inspirations and noble ambitions in the army would not explain Archibald. He had overcome those difficulties and losses years ago. Did the apparent loss of his sexuality as well in the army have anything to do with it? He had developed a very healthy relish for female flesh by the time he enlisted, and he was at a loss to explain precisely how he had misplaced it in the two years that followed. Part of it, he told himself this morning, not wishing to recall certain boozy events during those years, may have been that Edward and Clara were very nearly his only human contact afterward and the highly touted sexual urge seemed scarcely to exist for them. With Clara it seemed to be covered forever in her coat of spinsterhood, transformed into church suppers and good deeds for deserving people; with Edward it seemed to get wrapped up in the morning newspaper and discarded in the subway; and with all three of them it was, to a considerable extent, drowned in bourbon. Was there something hidden, something potentially explosive in all this? Archibald felt a curious lack of interest. Was his life really so abnormal and degraded that he had to agonize over it? He was sexless, jobless, and had no urges into the surrounding world of emotional risk. By what illusion of value, what myth, what superstition, were such peculiarities to be condemned? Did the virtual absence of a monastic tradition nowadays—at least as far as he was concerned—mean that one no longer had the right to live with the purity and simplicity of a monk?

Nobody would believe that sex is a fad, he reflected, precisely because it was such a fad. Such a fantastic, overpowering, and finally revolting fad. It crawled about their barracks floor like an enormous, soft alligator, chewing off ankles and legs at random. A kind of spiritual fastidiousness made him rebel to the point of vomiting in certain emotionally confusing situations. He had seen no physical beauty in those years even approaching the sight of Burlingame going over, and under, and through, the obstacle course, and Burlingame, with whom he had never had sex, was dead. What fitter place, therefore, to bury his sex, than with Burlingame? And so he had fasted as needed through the years to keep things under control; and if some urges remained in the depths of the night, he would copulate with Burlingame's ghost.

It was a perfectly tolerable life, after all. Why should he complain? If only it weren't for....

FOUR

Hannibal was really terrible today. Nora Melby must have gone out and left him there, waddling ceaselessly about her front door in the heat, barking to be let in. He was a short-haired, black-and-white mixture of bulldog and terrier with pink genitals and an explosive, high-pitched bark that could smash Archibald's awareness into hysterical fragments. And now the man crouched behind the shrubs at the edge of the lawn and watched the dog across the street, walking back and forth with stiff-legged senility.

He knew he shouldn't have let Hannibal draw him out here to spy on him through the bushes. It only made that bark more of an obsession—and what if someone saw him crouching there?—but he couldn't help it. He was finishing breakfast—though it was now early afternoon—when Hannibal began in earnest. He tried to shut it out. Impossible. It grew and filled his consciousness, like the dog that Faust brought into his study that turned out to be Mephistopheles in disguise.

I could skip across the street, he thought, and toss him a ball of hamburger with a core of broken glass.... Too risky. Not in the daylight. Better in the evening. Better in the fall in the early darkness. He had the glass ready in the cellar.

To think that he'd had Hannibal himself in the cellar last spring! Coaxed him in with a bit of hamburger with the firm intention of braining him with an old table leg. But the dog looked up at him with such soft brown eyes, such manifest sensitivity and intelligence...he couldn't. He knew he would falter and make a howling mess of it. The dog was so ugly at a distance, with patches of mange and one ear—chewed in a fight probably—flopping sideways, that he had been totally unprepared for such charm, and the chance was lost forever. For the dog sensed what was on the man's mind and would never go near him again.

Archibald would have to do Hannibal in for his own sanity, he realized that. Sweethill had a leash law and strict legislation against canine nuisances. Archibald knew. He had been though it all with Geller's dog, Twinky, five years ago. It was too much—the repeated calls of complaint to the town dog officer, the fines, the suspicions, the ill-feelings. He was not up to that any more. Better this way....

"Archie Bromley! So there you are!"

Archibald wheeled around, and there on the lawn, not six feet from where he stood, tall and slender in her dark dress and veil of mourning, was Gladys Worthington. She was between him and the house. There was no escape. He looked at her in silence.

"I rang your doorbell, and there was no answer, and your car was there. So I walked around the house.

It's familiar, Archie. I used to play here."

"Hello, Gladys."

She had large hazel eyes, a long face, a high round forehead framed by a veil and a heap of auburn hair. With her turned-up nose and her wide, friendly lips, she was still pleasant-looking, almost attractive still. Her skin was beginning to hang loose under her upper arms, but her body seemed firm, her bosom full. Why had she never married? Why do tribes, peoples sometimes, for no apparent reason, die from the face of the earth?

"I wanted to see you, Archie. I thought you might be at Priscilla Cameron's funeral. I thought I might see you there. But I shouldn't have expected it. I should have known that you wouldn't have troubled."

"Gladys, I...." He raised his head, tilted it to one side with his dark thick eyebrows arched in appeal and the palms of his hands turned outward.

"I know. You have nothing to say. Not to me. Not to anyone any more. But why? I don't understand it. You used to have so much to say. You were so full of life, interested in so many things. So funny, so kind. We all thought you were so great, Archie, even when you came back on vacation from that school."

"Gladys, let's not go over...."

"No, we won't go over it. You only want to be left alone. And I'm bothering you. But an old woman has just died who thought you had something wonderful, thought you *were* something wonderful, and you couldn't even go to pay your last respects to that woman who had done so much for you, found so much more in you than you ever found in yourself. No, you couldn't go because you had other more important things to do here, crouching in these bushes."

Archibald took a step to the side, toward the house,

but she stepped to the same side and remained blocking his way.

"No, you're not going to go just yet. I have one more thing to say. I knew you could do things that I didn't understand, but they worked and everyone could see that they worked. So when you came back from the army and didn't talk to anybody or see anybody, not even your oldest friends, I thought you must know what you were doing and that I just didn't understand it, and after a while I probably would understand it, and you would come out of it, and things would be as they were. But I never understood, and nobody ever understood, and you never came out of it. And now finally I do understand and know what it really is. You're just completely selfish and don't care about pleasing anybody but your own unhappy, ingrown self. You're not human at all, Archie. You're a monster. Maybe that's what you always were."

"Gladys...."

She was stopped short by the tone of agony in his voice.

"...I'm sorry, Gladys."

Her eyes opened wide, frightened by what she had done. Then they narrowed as a bitterness seemed to shadow her face. Then tears began in them, and she turned from him and walked briskly across the lawn, over a corner of the flagstoned terrace, which clattered under her high heels, and out into the street.

Wordless with such people, I bring on wordlessness in them finally, Archibald thought, as he followed in her steps across the lawn and stood on the terrace, looking at the space between two shrubs where she had vanished into the street. It would now be empty. At the moment he couldn't remember exactly what she had said. (It would come back to him, he knew, in excruciating detail at some future time, unpredictably, five minutes or five years hence.) All he had was a strong feeling that something had gone very wrong—with the day, with his life, with his project for killing Hannibal—he could not tell what.

Hannibal had stopped. Mrs. Melby must have come home and let him in. Archibald realized that he didn't care where the dog was and felt relieved of a burden.

But something was wrong with that—the relief of not caring any more about Hannibal. He must take stock. He was in danger of some kind—danger perhaps of sinking to a depth where even he would be swallowed.

He decided to have a glass of iced tea on the terrace and afterwards to have a look at the big elm in the southeast corner and decide whether it had to come down.

But he had looked at the elm a dozen times already and he knew perfectly well it would have to come down, knew that it had been diseased for years and was dead, thoroughly dead and rotten inside, and hazardous to every passer by, and if something, something drastic, wasn't done about it at once, a piece of it might fall off and maim or kill somebody.

He stood in anguish and looked around at the house, the mammoth trees. If there had been no inherited money, no easy place, no home to come to; if Edward and Clara had not been willing—eager even—to take him in and take care of him, then maybe he could have broken this silence that settled on him like the heat of a sultry evening, behind which the storms formed....

No, that was too easy. It lay in the three of them,

not in stones, trees, nor bank accounts, nor even in sultry evenings. There was something.... Gradually he became aware of something old and dark in his mind that he had always half known was there—an ancient suspicion that sloshed about down there, like the bilge in a slaver, crossing to Charleston from the Gold Coast, or like the oil left in the tank of an old oil truck, heaving about in the darkness when the truck has finished its deliveries in Sweethill and roars homeward.

FIVE

The sick suspicion...was about Clara and Edward—he could sense it—and this place, this world they had created for themselves and for him. And ancient. He could feel how ancient it was. He sat down heavily, almost crumpling the light aluminum terrace chair under him and forgetting about the iced tea he was going to make. Then suddenly he remembered the day over forty years ago on the same lawn when it began. He was sure of it. He must have been three or four years old. He had been crying—or had he only wanted to cry? His mother, or the maid, or perhaps Edward—not Clara, because she was only two years older than he—must have reprimanded him; and he sat in front of a large maple tree—now only a faint hollow in the ground between the petunias and azaleas, where the stump had been drawn out a dozen years ago—and back there when the tree was alive, something quiet and stupendous had happened. Reality—everything, the whole sensuous presence of things, seemed to modulate into a different tonality, seemed, without actually tearing, to heave, ripple and reveal things, dark and colorless, behind itself. It was then that he first acquired a belief that he now realized he had never entirely relinquished: that this whole scene surrounding him and everything in it was somehow arbitrary, merely put there, like a painted backdrop in a play. And if that were so, then somebody must have put it there. And if someone put it there, that someone must have had a purpose; and if that backdrop had deluded him until now into thinking that it was real and permanent, then that very delusion must have been the purpose.

He might not, of course, have reasoned so carefully at the age of three or four, but he decided now, at the age of 44, that these must have been the essential logical connections. And the logic went further. If someone was deluding him, that is, lying to him with things, placing things before him that were not really there, then the purpose of doing that must have been like the purpose of other lies told to him. Perhaps lying was something very new to him at that time. Perhaps it was not a reprimand, but a lie told to him that had brought tears to his eyes. And the purpose of this lie, he must have seen, had been to get him to do something someone wanted him to do. This would account for his clear memory of being convinced at the time that the motive for deluding him had been to get him to behave.

Didn't his mother and father say things to one another that they did not wish him to hear, things that they stopped talking about when he came into the room? Too much ice cream was bad for him—so his mother said. But was it true, or did she only say that because for some other reason she didn't want him to eat any more just then? So it was his mother and father who were fabricating reality. And Edward, who was fourteen at the time and already starting highschool before he, Archibald, had begun school of any kind— Edward must have been a party to it too, he must have known.

He wanted to run to tell Clara, who was with a playmate on the back porch, but he hesitated and decided not to for two reasons. First, Clara seemed to have a very slight regard for anything he said to her, and this was especially so whenever she had a playmate with her. And second, although she was a lot closer to him in age and every other way than anyone else in the family, she was still two years older than he. She was one of *them*. She might, therefore, have been a party to the fabrication, and at this point it seemed very important to him, not to let anyone like that know that he knew too. That was his one source of power: that he saw through their machinations and they didn't realize it. As long as they continued believing that he was fooled, then it was not he, but they, who were being fooled. They would be satisfied with what they had done. They would not think of doing something more powerful and dangerous that might obliterate him completely.

Archibald could remember how profoundly troubled he had been by his discovery, his conjecture. In a sense, it had determined his whole life. He was not sure that he had ever gotten free of it and of the tormenting doubts it engendered. Of particular importance was the separation from Clara that it seemed to enforce. It took her from him and placed her irrevocably with Edward, and to this day, although he knew better, although he understood matters perfectly well with his adult mind, he still kept slipping back into this child's mentality, and when he did so, he believed that now, at this very hour, Edward and Clara were still fabricating this house, lawn and garden so that he would behave himself in their absence.

He got up from the creaky little chair and paced about the terrace. Why did he keep falling into this trap? Another thought came to devastate him. Maybe Edward and Clara were pushing him into it, pushing him back into this childishness.

When he had come back from the army disoriented, devastated by Burlingame's death, and drinking heavily, they had been so kind, so eager to take him in. Something about them had made him uneasy. Before he went away the three children had their rooms on the third floor. Since his mother's death when he was twelve, the large bedroom, the "master bedroom," on the second floor over the livingroom had been unoccupied. His father had moved into the room over the front hall. The only other rooms on the second floor were the guest suite over the dining room and library and a large servant's room and bathroom on a back staircase over the kitchen. When he returned, he was vaguely shocked to discover that Clara had occupied the master bedroom. Edward had moved into the room his father had used next to it. It seemed only logical that he should move onto the second floor too. They would still want to have space ready for guests, so he moved into the room over the kitchen, the servant's room. In a strange way that seemed to define his position.

They were so glad to have him there, they said. But their very kindness and indulgence of his helplessness seemed to thrust him back into that helplessness, that agony of doubt and childishness from which he had never completely emerged. They were glad to have him there, but they were glad also— weren't they?—to have him safely tucked away with his own bedroom beyond the rear staircase and the two doors that led to his section. If he had kept his room on the third floor, he would have used the main stairs and passed through their part of the house regularly. The very design of things had conspired to keep him in his place.

No, it was not the design of things! He mustn't think that way! He must grow up! They had no sinister control over reality. Wasn't the house there before they were? No, no, only before he was! Even Clara had been born before this house was built. Dear God, he must try, try to see them, not with the eyes of the child as limitless inhuman powers but as ordinary flesh and blood like himself with ordinary passions, lusts....

Lusts! He thought of Clara and how she was always so neat, so carefully made-up and immaculate, even in the house. He had never since childhood seen her in any state even remotely approaching undress. Had Edward? Surely Edward, whose door was a scant three feet from hers....

Archibald stood still and his body stiffened, as if to withstand a wave on an ocean beach, when yet another huge thought came in upon him. Were Clara and Edward incestuous lovers? He had known it, half known it, long before this, hadn't he? It was the only hypothesis that accounted for the strange goings-on—for their welcoming him in order to make their menage seem credible and innocent, and for their keeping him at a distance, so that they could go on having their hours together undisturbed. He clutched the back rung of the chair he had been sitting in. He wanted to lift it, fling it.... It was strange how enraged and how calmed he felt at the same time. Calmed because with this sickening thought he had at last discovered what had gone so horribly wrong and had at last emerged from that thicket of childish illusions into this place of brutal fact. Enraged because, as before, but now even more disgustingly, he had been lied to, he had been cheated. Was she not closer to him in age—and in spirit—than to Edward, and therefore, if anyone's, rightfully his? He was being kept for show so that they could enjoy their pleasures with fewer questions asked, and for that petty little aim they had taken it upon themselves to destroy his life, soothing him all the while with nauseating pieties and sickening sentimentalities. He leaned carefully, meditatively, but with both trembling hands on the back of the little chair, which creaked alarmingly but held its shape.

Well, then, they would suffer for it.

Burn for it.

SIX

An orange Volkswagen swerved into the parking lot of Blake's Pond in Stoneyville, found a place, and out stepped Archibald. He walked a few steps in the direction of the bridge over the waterfall, then stopped, turned, and looked at his car. Salamander orange, he said to himself, the color of the broad jagged stripes on his friend, George Kaskin's salamanders. And the macadam surface of the parking lot, vaguely shimmering and liquescent in the August sun, was the color of their bodies, as they darted in and out among the rocks and ferns in Kaskin's wire enclosure. The sight made him understand why "Salamander" meant "fire" in Medieval alchemy. He had read that but never understood it. What had fire and this particular color to do with each other? The answer was disarmingly simple, almost naive. Kaskin's salamanders *looked* like fire when they darted about with their orange stripes crinkling and flashing.

Rage had begin to lead a life of its own in him. The fire was for them, Edward and Clara. He would see to it. He would not forgive them the twenty-four years he had spent, crippled in his spirit because it was in that form that they found him convenient. This was his last chance before age and decrepitude carried all before it. He must make the break, break out. Into what? What had he wanted? What was out there to find? Amazing how day linked with day—how many days? 5000? 10,000?—making such a pleasant, smooth path to oblivion. Lies. Everything they told him, lies. Nothing what it seemed. The salamanders seemed to be fire but were only lizards, and the anger nauseating him, that was only a lizard too, writhing in him. Where was there a crumb of truth in all this? For he had always imagined that it was to discover a truth in things that he was here on earth.

Was the truth, then, that he was no more than a collection of mean appetites and petty obsessions, slowly turning to a vegetable as a preliminary to shriveling completely and blowing away in the wind? Then he would at least find that was so. He must find out about arson. The library. Everything he needed was in the Sweethill Public Library, small but well-selected, only a short walk from the house. He loved browsing there, where no one could talk to him and he need talk to no one. Books, books on every subject imaginable had been almost his sole life for more than two decades.

He walked past the ducks gathered around a little girl and her parents and their bag of breadcrusts. But if that was the truth, why bother to find it out? They were pleasant enough, Edward and Clara, and every bit as useful to him as he to them. Why should he care about what they did in her bed, or his? Whatever it was must be pretty well used up by now. Clara was right, Edward looked terrible. When she said that this morning, had she been complaining about not getting what she wanted from him last night? It's the same in all marriages, so he had heard. The woman's appetite goes right on increasing as the man tires, fails. Worse when the wife is a lot younger, as Clara with Edward. With him and Clara, it would have been better, might have lasted a little longer....

Why not go on this way? They would be home soon. (Blake's Pond was only a five minute drive from the house on Clairmont Street. He could walk it easily, but with Nora Melbys and Gladys Worthingtons roaming the streets the car was better.) They would get out the bourbon and relax on the terrace and after a while Clara would make dinner—TV dinners usually—and another bourbon when they sat down to eat and a last nip "for the boys" as they washed up afterwards. If a few dishes got broken, they could be replaced.

What would his friend think of these revelations—George Kaskin, wild-eyed and bearded, who was a Communist—or so he claimed—and owned seven salamanders? He had recognized Archibald on the subway two years ago. A stranger in the seat ahead had twisted around and thrust his pop-eyed face at him and said, "Archibald Bromley, 218th Parachute Training Battalion, Fort Bragg. You were the squad leader in my first jump a couple of weeks before they let you out."

Archibald had been overwhelmed with delight and became garrulous with a stranger for the first time in over a decade. They got out at the same stop and had a beer together, the first of many. They had met every month or two since—brief, circumscribed meetings, usually in bars. Kaskin was Archibald's one connection with the outside world—his secret connection. Edward and Clara had only met him once: when Kaskin's communism and Clara's religion had threatened to become an explosive combination. She seemed to resent this intrusion from Archibald's other life—and was not at all interested in hearing about him. So he became, as it were, a part of Archibald's inner lone personality.

Yes, why not go on, leave things as they were? Hadn't he hurt them at least as much as they him? Clara disliked the mention of Kaskin, no doubt because of the bad time Archibald had given her when he got out of the army, the tauntings...the rhymes he repeated to her, like Burlingame's version of Hickory Dickory Dock:

> Huggery, buggery, snot,
> The whore fell off the cot.
> The cot was broke.
> The whore got up.
> Huggery, buggery, snot.

And the tirades....

"O yes, Clara, you're quite right. I should be proud that I risked my life for my country. I suppose that's alright to say, if you know what *my country* means, if it means anything at all, and if you can get the phrase defined in some way that doesn't make you lose your appetite, some way that can make you forget what it does to Negroes and what it did to German and Japanese cities.... But then you still have this problem. You've attached your ripcord to the wire. You're standing there near the open door 500 feet above the ground, a green blur of trees and fields rushing past the opening, and guys head of you, jumping out into that blur, one, two, three, and when your turn comes, you're going to jump too. But why? Why are you going to do that insane thing, against all logic and every law of survival? Because you love your country? Why, Clara, even if anything like that existed or was conceivable, it wouldn't move you one millimeter closer to that door.

"What then? Why are you going to jump? Because you are afraid not to? Afraid of a court martial for cowardice? The firing squad? They don't execute people for that any more, Clara. Then maybe you jump because you want to keep your good name, because you care so much about what other people say about you that you will put your own skin in jeopardy just to keep them saying the right things? Some people actually do jump for that reason, Clara, but for that to be the reason, the motive, don't they have to be the most insipidly conventional people you could imagine? Don't they have to be completely lacking in self-respect, respect for what they themselves think about anything?

"So if you are honest about it, it comes down to this: if you set any value at all on your life, your existence, your thoughts, you're not going to go through that opening. But there are the guys ahead of you going through it, and you know perfectly well you're going to too. And there's only one way to do it. You've got to discover and have to realize clearly and exactly that your life is worthless, means nothing at all, and you don't care in the slightest whether it ends at that moment or not. That's the only way you are going through that door. Your sweet stinking country has nothing to do with it."

"O Archie, dear, I wish you had more faith! You seem to want to take the joy out of everything."

"She's right, Arch," said Edward. "Aren't you laying it on a bit thick? This patriotism thing has been big all through history. *Pro patria mori*, and all that."

"I've an idea you might want to think about, Edward, my brilliant scholar and quoter of Latin. Don't hurry to it, though. Wait till you are ready to do some thinking."

"We don't need so much sarcasm, little brother, Tell us your idea."

"O. K. You say patriotism has been this big thing through history. Faith in the goodness of the cause, aspirations for the Fatherland. All that stuff. Let's take the Roman Army—and think about this little proposition: the Roman Army didn't conquer the world on faith or hope, but on despair. Picture it, a crack Legion drawn up at attention, glittering in the sun. Perfectly equipped, of course. Trained, to be sure. But the equipment was nothing special, and the training would have gotten nowhere without the essential ingredient to work upon. Think of that, that essential force and quality of the Legion: inside of every man—what? Hopes? Fears? An ego even? Things like that make cowards of us, shrivel years of training in seconds when the heat's on. No, inside of every man, like a little, smooth, round, perfectly polished stone, the same hopelessness and unconcern, the same quintessential immutable spirit of total meaninglessness. That's what made them invincible!"

He was saying all this to Edward, but he was saying it to get at Clara, to get into Clara! Right there in Edward's jealous presence. Except that Edward wasn't jealous, not apparently so, either because he was too good a person to feel jealousy or too unsuspecting, too stupid. For the past twenty-four years—for their whole lifetimes even—Archibald had been unable to make up his mind about Edward. And now he was proposing in his heart to murder Edward, to set the house on fire while he was in the incestuous embraces of their beloved sister and consummate their love by burning them to a single intertwined crisp.

He looked up. Ducks were quacking in panic and waddling in all directions from his blundering steps. A little blond girl in a blue playsuit was looking at him reproachfully. Hadn't he seen her before? Heavens! He had passed her right here a few minutes ago feeding those ducks, and had walked completely around the pond, lost in his thoughts, finding his way by reflex and not noticing a thing he had passed. And it was such a lovely spot.

How heedless could he be? He had condemned his brother and sister to death without the slightest shred of evidence against them. Clearly that must be the first order of business: to collect evidence. Get proof positive. He had some ingenuity, hadn't he? Tomorrow he must examine everything in their part of the house. Circumstantial bits. And then if that went well, he could build up to catching them in the act. The climax. Ha!

It did not occur to him right away that there might be no evidence. That would have been too cruel, after all this, for there to have been nothing. He was emotionally committed, like the totalitarian state that finds it difficult to discover that someone it has arrested may be innocent.

Archibald had climbed the rocks above the waterfall and seated himself on a ledge. The water, twisting and splashing among the stones, then collapsing upon itself ten feet below, suggested the motion of his thoughts: their headlong uncertainty. He broke off a twig from an overhanging branch, tossed it into the stream above the fall, and watched it bobbing nervously, now here, now there, as it approached the brink. He must be like that stick, ready to be carried anywhere, accept anything, even the enormous debilitating relief of their innocence.

SEVEN

"So you got up today after all, Archie!"
The pleased note was evident in Clara's voice when he emerged from the French doors of the library onto the terrace, where she was sitting.
"Where have you been?"
"Driving around."
"Pour yourself a drink."
"In a moment." He sat down in his usual chair opposite hers and looked at her carefully, more carefully than he had in years. Her lips were Cupid-bowed and full, like his own and unlike Edward's, and the bridge of her nose was continuous with her forehead, as in Ancient Greek statues of Aphrodite. Was that it? Or had he seen a portrait of her on an early Minoan platter with snakes twining in her arms? Something that an age of eyebrow plucking and permanent waves in her fading blond hair could never obliterate. The flared nostrils...the yellowish brown eyes, kindly, yet totally matter-of-fact, that seemed to gather strangeness with the years as the shadows around them deepened. Something austere. She would age well.
She returned his look. "I feel scrutinized."
Broad shoulders, he thought, fine breasts, a trim

belly—a sign of good muscles down there...slender legs...he shivered involuntarily, and his glance returned to the kindliness in her eyes, emphasized by little crow's feet.

"You look innocent enough."

"I'm too old to be innocent. Old as the stones in that wall today. That client interested in the Mills Corner site is the end.... Hey, Archie, what is this? Some kind of game? Stop looking at me that way and go get yourself a drink, dear, like a good boy."

He felt a quick little wave of rage and was uncertain for a moment what had caused it. The "dear" that she had used for him was the "dear" that one uses for a child. When she used it with Edward, that same word meant an equal. Everything was so different now than it had been even this morning. A veil had been torn off. Everything was naked now. No lightness of tone could cover things any longer. He would never trust himself again to refer to them openly, accusingly, as lovers, as he had this morning. That weapon, that playful device—like so many others, no doubt—had been taken from him with the tearing apart of things.

"You know, Clara, I'm not really a good boy. In fact—you may have noticed—I'm not even a boy at all any more. Your lovely sylphlike Ganymede has turned into a dirty old Satyr."

"For the beauties of the earth shall pass away, saith the Lord!"

Archibald looked over his shoulder. "Hello, Ed. Where did you come from?"

"The Cavern of Delights."

"The dispensary of ice cubes, bourbon, and swizzle sticks."

"Yea, verily!"

"Ice cubes, bourbon, and swizzle sticks," Archibald went on, "our Holy Trinity, with Father Bourbon in the central place, like the sun in the Solar System, surrounded by its planets, the ice cubes and swizzle sticks that would be nothing without it."

"Yea, verily!" Edward said with a touch of weariness, sinking into his chair and resting there, holding the large glass in his lap with both hands, then reaching with one of the hands for his pipe in an inner pocket.

"Why Eddie, I thought we were going to bandy high-sounding phrases, Biblical quotations...."

"It's been a long day, Arch."

"Archie, do you have any theory," said Clara briskly, "that might explain why for long periods you will have absolutely nothing to say to anybody and then suddenly you are like your old self, but even more so, bubbling with words, thoughts, innuendos?"

"No, no theories. It's too simple a matter for theory. Most of the time there is nothing to say, and when there is nothing to say, which is increasingly the case, I find, as life goes on, then I have formed an extraordinary habit. When there is nothing to say, I actually say nothing."

He knew that she tolerated his silences because she feared the manic states even more. Well, mustn't disappoint her.

"You're being facetious," she said. "Well, since you're so full of beans tonight, maybe I can get you to agree to go to the neighborhood party at the Contis with us on Friday. Yes? O lovely! And that reminds me. Did you go to Priscilla Cameron's funeral today?"

"No, I didn't."

He looked at Edward, who was looking into his glass, and he looked across the lawn to the honeysuckle where he and Gladys Worthington had stood earlier that afternoon. If he let himself sink now, he could not be sure of the consequences, so he decided to struggle against the shadow cast by Clara's question.

"No, the shovelfuls of dirt thudded on the lead box containing her dear rotting remains with neither my passionate secular presence nor my pious benedictions."

Clara uncrossed her legs and sat up rigidly.

"I don't know why you have to say things like that. Some of us believe that rituals like that mean something, even if you don't, and you might show a little respect for what other people believe. Are you afraid of something—that you have to be so arrogant about everything?"

"He's trying to be playful, Clara," said Edward, looking up and responding to the distress in her voice. "he doesn't mean any harm."

How quick he is to soothe her little feathers, thought Archibald. "He's right, Clara. Don't be offended by my cloddish—no pun intended—attempts to be funny, thudding on poor Priscilla's coffin. I know how hard it is to believe things like that..." he paused for as long as he dared, "...when everybody keeps assaulting your belief."

"It isn't everybody, Archie." said Clara. "You're the odd man out here."

"Am I, Ed?"

"I mean here in this town, this country," said Clara. "We haven't changed, in spite of all we've been through. The war, the peace marches...we're still the same people."

"God help us!" said Archibald.

"He will!" said Clara.

"Will He help you, help you two when you go to

meet Him, hand-in-hand, carrying the sins that you are carrying?"

"Keep it down, Arch. What's the matter with you? The whole neighborhood is going to hear you," said Edward almost in panic.

"Sorry," said Archibald. "I do seem to be having trouble, modulating my voice tonight, modulating it into the right key, the key that opens all mysteries. You're ready for another drink, Ed. Come. To the Cavern. Clara?"

"A small one for me, thanks. I'm going to see what's in the freezer."

The bar was in a small playroom off the library, and the brothers eyed each other, walking toward it."

"Are you alright, Arch? You seem, O, maybe a little troubled about something tonight."

"Yes, Ed, I *am* troubled about something." Archibald's voice was a little higher than usual and very clear and evenly pitched, giving an impression of careful precision and cold anger, and as he spoke, he observed Edward intently. "I'm troubled about you and Clara and what you do together."

Edward's eyes and mouth opened wide. He seemed to drift ahead for a moment, gulping air with his eyes fixed on nowhere, lazily, like a balloon wafted toward the doorway. Then he stopped short, turned abruptly to Archibald, who was a little shorter than he and who had also stopped, and said,

"What the Hell are you talking about?"

His voice shook in outward anger—somewhat pitifully, for anger was not a natural emotion for Edward—but inwardly the note, the sick quaver of guilt was unmistakable. Suddenly all the voices in Archibald's soul rang together at once in a thrilling chorus of exultation. Edward was caught. It was obvious, absolutely obvious.

But now Archibald was on the defensive and suddenly fearful, lest Edward discover that his brother knew his secret. He wasn't ready for that. Edward was too powerful. If they knew that he suspected, they might very well manage to have him put away. Archibald had no illusions about that. He knew very well the kind of figure he cut in the town, and he knew what it meant for a grown man, sound in body, to be unemployed for twenty-four years in the town of Sweethill.

"Yes, Ed." He did not dare to make his voice suddenly milder—that might arouse suspicion; in an inspired move he actually raised its pitch a little more, which gave it a faint suggestion of madness, which Edward could imagine that he had missed in Edward's previous sentence. "I'm troubled about how hard you and Clara seem to be working on these hot summer days. I think you do too much. You may not like this, but I have to say it—you and she aren't getting any younger, and as she herself said this morning, old buddy, you're beginning to show the wear a little. Yes, I confess, I have been a little troubled about that."

He felt gleeful in his agony, watching relief suffusing a soft radiance into Edward's face.

"That's awfully considerate of you, Arch."

"And you know, Ed," Archibald went on, his voice almost normal now as they arrived at the bar, "maybe you and Clara ought to take a little vacation and have a complete rest for yourselves for a couple of weeks."

"O Heavens, Arch, we're home enough; we wouldn't know what to do with ourselves here all day."

Archibald noted with satisfaction that Edward had returned to his habit of lumping himself and Clara easily together in the marital duplicate, showing how completely his alarm had subsided.

"No, Ed, I mean—take her off somewhere—to the Cape, maybe—and have yourselves a complete change for a couple of weeks. Go to the beach, take some boat rides, sit and bask in the sun. When you come back, you'll feel like new people."

"You do make it sound tempting. You'd come along, wouldn't you?"

"No, no. I don't need a vacation. I'm on vacation from one end of the year to the other. And that's part of getting away completely for you. Getting away from me too."

"Not a bit of it, Arch."

"Talk with Clara about it. See what she says."

"You know, I just might do that. You really are a sterling little brother to have thought of it."

They were still talking about the vacation when Clara appeared in the doorway.

"Soup's on, boys."

EIGHT

Clara had wheeled their TV dinners into the dining room on an antique tea wagon, and "the boys" came from the bar with a fresh round of bourbon. They all helped, setting out the place mats, silverware, and finally the dinners on their compartmented plates; and when they had turned out the lights, lit the candles, and sat down, Archibald gazed at his plate and thought tipsily.

What sort of mush is this?

He was glad he mostly cooked for himself—the meal this noon, and there would be a snack tonight, if he didn't drink too much and fall asleep.

"Sorry if it's not very elaborate tonight, boys. I just didn't feel up to very much on a day like today."

When was it ever elaborate? thought Archibald.

"Quite right, my dear," said Edward and took a healthy gulp of bourbon.

"Rest assured of one thing, Clara," said Archibald, "No matter what you do. No matter what culinary crimes you may commit or kitchen catastrophes you may perpetuate...."

They both looked up with anxiety in their faces, fearing lest he be growing manic again.

"...you will never sink to the level achieved by the cooks of the Queensbury Academy."

"Yes, the food seems to have gotten worse there in your time," said Edward.

"The War, dear. There was a war on," said Clara.

"Yes, indeed," said Archibald, "and old Wintergreen played that War for every penny it was worth. There was one dish we had at least once a week, a kind of creamed fish, the fish from the stink and slime of the Connecticut River. At their best, they would only have tasted of engine oil and sewage, but mucked up and festering in this greenish-yellow cream...you couldn't stay in the same room with it. One time the student waiter brought it on, and old Honest John Cingleton was presiding at the table, a young guy with this big raspy voice, who wasn't long for the place. I think he was gone the next year. And he looks down at this stinking mush and then he looks up at us and around at everybody, and 'Anybody want any of this?' he rasps."

Archibald responded, "'Waiter, take this back to the kitchen; nobody wants any.' That was a pretty unheard-of thing to do."

"I should think so," said Clara. "No wonder he didn't

come back next year."

"Food was a sensitive subject around there, and nobody was allowed to say anything about it because there was a war on and shortages and old Wintergreen was taking advantage of that and using food to balance the budget. So you had to be really careful what you said. One day we're at this other master's table—I forget whose—and my friend O'Connell is sitting beside me and these little black leathery pieces of meat are being passed out, and all of a sudden O'Connell says in this big loud voice, 'Quick, Bromley, kill it! It's moving! It's getting away!' That went straight to Wintergreen, and they put O'Connell in Group IV for that one remark."

"I guess with the War on, everybody was expected to do his bit," said Clara.

"You'd think they'd be able to take a little joke, though, wouldn't you?" said Edward.

"Thing was," said Archibald, "it was too good a joke. If it had been a dumb joke, they'd have said it was O. K. And if it had been outstandingly insipid, they'd have given O'Connell a little prize for saying something harmless."

"Whereas Archibald Bromley thinks that people ought to be given prizes only when they say things that are harmful and dangerous," said Clara.

Archibald looked at her gloomily, and her eyes flashed back. He decided to let the remark pass.

"I forget who it was," said Edward, "one of the modern critics—a favorite of old Hornsby's—said there was something terribly unpleasant about all great poetry. You see, your friend O'Connell was a great poet and so no one liked what he said and punished him for it. Dirty bastards, they punished him for it!"

"Ed, you're NOT going to have another bourbon

already!" said Clara. "Have your dinner first."

"No? Well...I suppose you're right." He slumped back into his chair, put down his glass, picked up his fork, and tentatively prodded his food.

"The days are getting shorter," said Clara. "It's getting dark already."

"And the planets are going," said Archibald.

"The what?" said Edward.

"The planets," said Archibald. "all but Venus. Venus is out there still, shining above the sunset. Venus, the goddess of love, twinkling over our destinies." He looked at Clara. Did she smile back at him? She must be tired of Edward after all these years. Hump, bump. Hump, bump, night after night—for how many years was it? God, he felt tipsy. "But they were all there earlier this summer. Even Mercury for a little while at first. But Mercury is hard to see. I'm not even sure I saw Mercury myself. It moves so fast, it was gone in a few days. Only eighty days in the Mercurial year. But the others—all four of the others—Venus, Jupiter, Mars, and Saturn—then afterwards, changing places, Jupiter, Venus, Saturn, and Mars—all strung out in a huge arc across the evening sky, sketching the plane of the ecliptic. And all continuously moving in that plane, a little different every night, among themselves and against the background of the fixed stars—Saturn moving very slowly, Jupiter less slowly, Mars faster, Venus faster still, and now and then, dancing among them in the same vast plane, fragments of moon, moving fastest of all. You should have come out on the front lawn or up into the third floor skylight with me to look at them. I asked you to come, told you you ought to see them, because there isn't going to be another display like that for eleven years. People spend all night, getting caught in traffic jams, stinking crowds, to watch a puny fireworks display, but the whole cosmos on display—they haven't got five minutes for that. And the way you are looking at me with your mouths hanging open, you're going to tell me you don't even remember me telling you about it."

"O Archie, dear, I *don't* remember you telling us about it—at least not so that we realized how strongly you felt about it."

"Yes, Arch, we just didn't know."

"If we'd known how strongly you felt about it," Clara continued, "we'd have been glad to come out with you."

That brazen, incestuous *we!!*

"Goddammit, do you think I give a fancy fiddler's fuck whether you come out and see the planets with me or not? I can see the planets perfectly well for myself. What I am talking about is you and whether you have any interest at all in what kind of a tremendous world you live in and in seeing what the world is really like."

"Well, if you don't stop using that kind of language, I'm going to take my dinner and my drink and go straight to my room and lock the door," said Clara.

"O come on, Clara, act your age, my dear," said Edward.

"Act my age! Well I never!"

"No, dear, just sit back down there and calm yourself. Archie isn't going to use language like that any more, are you, Arch? Come on now, both of you. Arch, you have all the time you want to read books from the library and think about things, and I know after all these years, you've got a much better education than I have, even though you only went to college for two months when you got out of the Service and

I went for four years. But you ought to be tolerant of us. Clara and I have been working pretty hard at our jobs over the years, and you've just been...well...you've been doing what you have to do—thinking, and looking at the stars, Saturn and Neptune...."

"I haven't been looking at Neptune," said Archibald, "because Neptune is invisible to the naked eye."

"Archie, you know what he means. Why do you have to be so nasty?"

"All I meant to say, Arch, was that you have time to read and think."

"While Ed and I are out working so you *can* read and think."

"Clara, your salary and Ed's combined wouldn't pay either the taxes on this place or the liquor bill. You know it and I know it, so why kid ourselves, when I can read the accounts as well as you? You're nothing but a glorified secretary, and Ed, if you ever asked that Yummy-Tummy Ice Cream Company for a living wage, they'd send you packing in three seconds."

"O!" cried Clara, as though that last barb had been plunged in her own breast.

Edward smiled faintly and gazed at Archibald with his beautiful eyes. "Arch, you know perfectly well the name of the company I work for. It's the Hendricks Ice Cream Company."

"Is it now, Ed! No, come on. You can't fool me. It's the Yummy-Tummy. We both know that. And you work there, not so that I will be able to read and think, but so that you won't *have* to read and think."

"That's right, Arch. That's quite true," said Edward, pushing his chair back and rising slowly to his feet. "You hit it right on the head." He turned and stumbled with his empty glass in the direction of the bar.

NINE

"You hit *him* right on the head!" Clara hissed as soon as Edward was out of the room. "You're going to kill that poor man, Archie. Have you no pity? Can't you see how terrible he looks, how he drinks? Going on like that about his job! He's too nice a person even to *want* a living wage. Look, he's hardly touched his dinner."

Remorse swept into Archibald's delirium. He had been riding so high. His new aggressiveness and loquaciousness, trying to discover the truth about their relationship, had exposed their weakness astonishingly—as though he had tried to peel a bandaid from a man's chest and half the man, who was made only of papier-mâché, had come with it. His first impulse had been to romp a little in the mess, but Clara had brought him to his senses.

"I'm sorry," he said. When had he said that before, today?

"And so you should be. Wasn't once enough? I mean, haven't we been through this—or something like this—before?"

"Yes, I know what you're thinking," he said.

"That summer, after you graduated from Queensbury but didn't get into Harvard. That awful summer you spent arguing with Dad."

"And now Ed is there instead of him."

"And I was there in the first place instead of mother."

"But Archibald has always been Archibald."

She smiled. "It's hard to be put in a role that you can't fill. I didn't know what to do. Still don't when you two get going. Don't let you and him be like you and father. Let him live, Archie."

"Mirrors within mirrors, illusions...illusions! Don't be maudlin, Clara. Don't blame me for father's heart attack. Our Father Who Art in Heaven, I'm not to blame for the failure of your pump. He did what was in him to do. And so will Ed. But don't worry about Ed. Substantial fellow, Ed. Solid. You ought to know, Clara, what's in him to do. You must have a lot bigger influence over him than I do. Get him to stop drinking so much. Use your feminine wiles."

She looked at him coldly, rigidly. He had been pretending to be somewhat drunker than he was.

"I don't see what my feminine wiles—if I have any, and I'm sure I don't—would have to do with Edward's health."

"You might get him to cut down.... Clara, how come you and Ed—how come you never got married?"

Archibald couldn't help it. He was growing silly, and in that new state he was pleased by the triple meaning of his question. The last "you" could be either singular or plural, and as plural, it meant either, "Why did you two never marry other people?" or "Why did you never marry each other?"

"Nobody has ever asked me that before. But you've already answered it yourself. You do what's in you to do. I saw a lot of it when mother died, Archie. It was horrible. Cancer is such a hideous disease. She just wasted away to nothing. Weighed less than 80 pounds at the end. And she was so young and lovely. She was all that was sweet and gentle and in love with life—like Ed. You and I are like Dad—something's cruel in us. He and his medicine—his surgery—it seemed so dumb and useless, and even seemed—I know this sounds crazy—it even seemed to be what blighted her. You have that blighting quality, Archie. Maybe I do too, and that's why.... But why are you asking me all these things? You've really had me under investigation since you came out on the terrace, haven't you? What's up? I'll bet it has something to do with those nasty innuendos you keep making about Ed and me, about how Ed and I are.... I think you almost believe something like that, and you know, Archie, that's so disgusting and crazy that, if it's true, I really think you had better start counting your marbles."

If it's true...if it's true—kept echoing in Archibald's mind. Good God, he thought, she's admitting that it might be true! But those thoughts were almost obliterated by the profound embarrassment he felt at the same time. He really had to admire the way she turned his enquiry—his whole probing apparatus—back on himself. Did that argue for her innocence, or for her shamelessness?

Edward came into the room.

"Ed, pour some of that into Archie's glass. Please, dear—please, Ed! You've had enough."

"Excellent idea, my dear! Share and share alike, I always say. There's the glass, Arch. Now, if you'll be so good as to pick it up and pour some into yours—an operation of some complexity, better performed by yourself at this time of night. Clara, I want you to know that this is a sterling young man with a most noble and gener...most noble and generous heart. It may be that he has made me examine my worth, my ulti...ultimate worth as a citizen and as the head of a household, as the IRS designates me, a little more searchingly and carefully than I might have been moti...motivated to do on my own this evening; but nevertheless I want to testi...testify and offer a concrete piece of evidence for his noble and gener...heart. A short while ago, my dear, Archibald said that you and I should go on a vacation together—just you and

I together—to the wild excitements of the Cape—in recognition of our time in harness, our ef...efforts in the marketplace."

"A vacation?" said Clara. "Why I think that's a marvelous idea. Archie, you *are* a dear. You *are* so sweet.... And now, boys, shall we clear the table?"

She stood up, but before she could begin gathering the dishes, Edward was by her side.

"Yes," he said, "an inspired suggestion, insp...but first let us properly celebrate—celebrate our coming vacation. For our celebration, let us—the celebrities—march to our destiny—our destiny over there." His hand lunged in the direction of the buffet across the room. "Let us march there arm in arm, showing our sodality—our solidarity. Put your arm in mine, now, dear. That's right. And now as we march, let the organ play." They set off across the carpet, and his husky baritone intoned,

> Here comes the bride.
> All step aside!

Clara leapt from Edward's side, as though stung by a viper up his sleeve. "Drunken pig! It's time you went to bed. O Ed, Ed, why do you do this? Why is this happening? ...Archie! Why are you just sitting there, glowering at us? All right, you two, we're going to sit back down at the table and have it out, once and for all."

She went back to her chair, and Edward, who had been swaying gently back and forth, stunned by her outburst, made it softly to his.

She placed her forearms on the table—an unusual gesture for her—and intertwined the fingers of both hands. "I was never married. I never felt that I'd make a very good mother to anyone—not after my own mother said some of the things she said to me before she died. But I seem to have ended up with children after all, my own brothers. Archie, will you please explain yourself and say exactly what's on your mind? Something's on your mind. I know it, and I want to know what it is. Ed, have you been aware this evening that there's something on Archie's mind?"

"Yes...aware."

Archibald's eyes, deep-set under their dark, thick brows and scarcely visible in the candlelight, which was beginning to gutter, moved methodically back and forth from one to the other.

"Well, Archie, out with it. I think you know perfectly well that Ed and I have been honest with you. When you came home from the army in the state you were in, came home to Ed and me, we made this a home for you. O, it's yours too. But what would you have done without us? You ask a lot of questions, but have you ever asked yourself that one? And what would you still do without us? Because a lot of people would say that you're even worse off now than you were then. The only place you'll go, Archie, is to the library, where if you meet anybody, you don't have to talk to them. Ed and I still have to do almost all the shopping."

Yes, they were like an old married couple in the supermarket, him pushing the basket in his dark suit with vest and watchchain and straw hat while she put things into it, dressed in her light blue coat and white pumps, the same things year after year. Had he heard someone say that? Or had he only thought it, dreamt it? He felt a sea of illusions beginning to engulf him.

"So maybe you should be honest with us. You've

started making disgusting jokes about Ed and me rather insistently, and now tonight—I don't know what you've been doing, but poor Ed's upset and I'm beginning to climb the walls. So what's on your mind, Archie?"

"What's on my mind? Illusions. Illusions are on my mind." He paused and looked carefully at them both one last time, just to be absolutely sure what, if anything, was expected of him and how badly, if at all, he was cornered. Edward, nodding, clinging to the last remnant of his consciousness, was of no concern. He wouldn't remember a thing tomorrow. As for Clara, she was probably the soberest of the three—which would hardly clear her of the charge of drunkenness. In any case, Archibald sensed that she had discharged her lightning and was beginning to cloud over already. She was obviously more interested in making statements than in asking questions, and it was plain that she didn't really think that Archibald had anything substantial on his mind at all. She probably didn't even think he was *in* his right mind. Then why trouble to disabuse her?

"Illusion, dear brother and sister, is the stuff of our lives and the sign of our times. Nothing is what it seems. This room, this house, us—nothing is necessary. Nothing indubitable. From my point of view, you two might just be inventing it for me, putting it on, like a stage manager, putting on scenery, or like a painter, putting paint on the scenery...."

He was right, Clara hadn't murmured.

"And this illusion—this sense of illusion that is the stuff of our lives and the sign of our times and of the consciousness of everyone in our times and in our culture—is essentially an *historical* phenomenon. There was no such sense of illusion riddling experience from top to bottom in most other times and places. Medieval Europe, for example, was such a time and place—and modern Russia. In places and times like that, holy places, holy times..."

"Holy! Russia?" said Clara.

"...there is no illusion, no sense of it; which is to say that except for a few heretics, like the Albigensians, or a few dissidents, who are suppressed with remarkable cruelty, it was all the same illusion and there was no breaking it." He was speaking in a mystical, literary voice with a pseudo-Harvard accent. "Everything was what it seemed. The loving older brother and sister generously remaining single so that they can take care of their poor addled younger brother, were what they seemed to be, and the salamanders running around in their cages with the orange stripes on their gray bodies coruscating, so that they looked like fire, *were* fire. There is no denying it. We cannot tell the alchemists that it wasn't so because the alchemists are dead and can't hear us anymore. They are dead, like the boy in the poem, raped by the King of the Elves, and no one can ever teach him our comfortable interpretation of what happened, that it was only the wind in the reeds, and so no one can ever deny him his experience as he visualized it because he is dead, dead forever."

Edward's lids had almost covered his eyes, but Clara's eyes were flashing.

"Archie, I hate it when you go on like this. Nothing is settled and nothing makes any sense, and I'm going to bed. Come on, Ed, get out of that chair and come to bed. Or else...."

She stopped suddenly and looked at Archibald with her mouth open.

"Archie, would you see that he gets out of that chair and goes to bed? Because you know as well as I do

that if he sleeps like that, he'll feel terrible in the morning. Would you mind doing that? And I guess we'll have to ask you to wash up—or at least put things in the washer—and set out the breakfast things."
"I'd be glad to."
"You're a dear. Did I cut you off in what you were saying? What were you saying? I'm so tired. Could you tell me just briefly what you were saying?"
"I was thinking of the first line of the only poem I ever read at Queensbury that I liked or understood. It summarizes in one short sentence everything I was trying to say." He paused.
"Well?"
"The pure products of America go crazy."
"Who?"
"Us!"
"O Archie—sleep well—if you can." And she went off to bed.

TEN

Archibald sat at the kitchen table and listened for the sound of Clara's Cadillac. He heard its door open and then slam and then a moment later the whine of the starter, which died unnoticed as the engine burst into life. Then the engine too, all eight large cylinders of it, died into a murmur so faint that he could not be certain he heard it at all. It didn't matter, for presently he heard the sound he was waiting for: the crunching of the gravel under the tires as the mammoth vehicle glided smoothly around the grape arbor and out into the street. Clara was on her way to Minor, Benton, and Furtz, the downtown realtors. Edward had already left for his ice cream company, none the worse, apparently, for last night's bourbon.

Archibald brought his dishes to the sink. No eggs this morning. He would be able to load everything directly into the dishwasher without first removing the clotted egg yolk from his plate with a wire brush and cold water. He had decided to eat and drink less for a while, and already, after skipping his snack last night and paring down his breakfast today, he felt leaner, lighter, and more vigorous. Today he would investigate the bedrooms.

Strange how familiar the new state of affairs had become after only one day. It was difficult to believe that the first explosive suspicion—detonated somehow, he was still not sure exactly how, by Gladys Worthington's tirade—was only yesterday. Perhaps because he had already suspected for months, years, without realizing it. But also because the drunken scene with Edward and Clara last night, the testing, the probing, seemed like a gulf so large that anything that happened before it had to be ancient.

Perhaps he would find nothing, no corroboration of any kind in the house. What, after all, could he possibly find? Surely Clara, at least, would be very careful not to leave any clues for her little brother and the cleaning woman, who came every Wednesday morning. But what did he need to find? Didn't he have conclusive evidence from last night? When he woke this morning (about fifteen minutes before Clara called him) he had been convinced that he did. But now in the full blaze of daylight and the critical consciousness that went with it, he wasn't so sure.

Edward's angry defensiveness when he thought Archibald might suspect had seemed obvious enough. But even there—how could one be sure that one was not forcing the raw happenings into a mold of arbitrary imagination that might have nothing whatever to do with the actual nature of the happenings? You go to a party and, as one of the dishes, you see white slivers of something molded into a shimmering jelly. Meat probably. Surely not slivers of cabbage or cole slaw. But what meat? Chicken, lobster, crabmeat? Edward's defensiveness *when he thought Archibald might suspect*, wasn't that forcing Edward's reaction into the mold of one's own conception? Maybe Edward, totally innocent, was only wondering angrily what his crazy brother was going to accuse him of now.

And the case against Clara, if there was any case at all, was even more dubious. The only way to find out what kind of meat was in the jelly was to bite into it.

Into the bedrooms, then! Archibald turned the dishwasher handle into the "lock" position and pressed the "full cycle" switch. And as the engine rumbled and the water gurgled, he went out of the kitchen and through the pantry, and passing the dining room on his left and beyond it the bar—last evening's Cavern of Delights—he strode through the coatroom and out into the main hall. Quite a magnificent house the old man planned, thought Archibald: quite a reward for a pair of deft hands. He remembered Konrad Adenauer, the West German Chancellor, on TV:

"You Germans have socialized medicine," said the reporter accusingly.

"Nah, ya," said the old man, "you Americans have a privileged class of doctors."

So far, Archibald was on a familiar path, traversed so exactly so many times, he wondered that there was not a path worn on the main hall rug. Then he remembered that about five years ago they had had the rug changed precisely because there *was* a path worn on it.

But when he turned from this path and mounted the main stairs to the second floor, it was like venturing into a wilderness, the robber-infested hills. The stairs were the first thing you saw when you came through the front door, so he had seen them several times a day now, continuously, well into the third decade. But when was the last time he had climbed them? When, since his first weeks there and the move from his child's room on the third floor to the servant's room on the second, reached by the back staircase, had he *ever* climbed them?

Of course, he had used them occasionally over the years to carry out certain chores: in autumn sometimes to fasten the storm windows on the inside that he had put on from a ladder outside, and in the spring to unfasten them—though even at these times Edward usually did the inside work. And not too many months ago he had used them to replace a faulty float valve in Edward and Clara's toilet. But times like that didn't count. When he used the front stairs at such times, it was not as Archibald Bromley: it was as a *workman*. He had the same tentative blundering air of a man in dirty overalls with calloused fingers and filthy fingernails who is permitted among the mirrors at Versailles in order to repair the plaster in a ceiling. Never had he mounted that staircase as one of the three proprietors whose name, duly notarized and with all the proper seals and stamps, appeared on the deed on file in the County Seat.

When he had fixed the toilet, Clara's door and Edward's, next to one another in the opposite corner of the upper hall, had been closed, and it would have been unthinkable to have tried them to see whether they were locked. For such a thought would have violated an essential clause in the code by which the three of them lived: an unwritten code (for there is no need to write what is self-evident) of absolute and inviolable privacy.

And today also, the doors were closed.

Archibald went to a little window in the hall and looked out over the driveway, save for his Volkswagen, empty, as it would remain until late this afternoon.

He went into the bathroom, whose door was ajar—he noted just how much, so that he could leave it in exactly the same position when he left. There was a shiny pink shower curtain, bunched up at the head end of the bathtub, that he had never seen. The whole room had been redone about fifteen years ago with beige cabinets and woodwork, aquamarine tiles above the bathtub, and a large aquamarine counter, with flecks of gold, around the sink. Little stylized beige and aquamarine fish swam in the creamy wallpaper, and the wall above the sink was all mirror. Clara and Edward could stand together before it, admiring themselves.... Directly over the sink were two panels in the large mirror. Archibald took the little knob on one of these between his thumb and forefinger and slid it cautiously back. An old-fashioned shaving bowl, shaving brush and double-edged safety razor came into view. He closed it and slid the other panel open. Lipsticks, an eyebrow pencil, and some other items whose use he did not understand.

This is getting nowhere, he murmured, shut the panel and went out into the hall, forgetting about the position of the door.

He paused again in the middle of the hall, looking at the two doors. Then, pressing his lips together, he strode to Edward's door, opened it, and stepped into the room.

He couldn't believe what he saw. He seemed not to have entered a room actually used by a living human being but to have blundered into a museum of some kind—"Longfellow House" or "Lincoln's Birthplace."

"Washington Slept Here."

Washington, maybe, thought Archibald, but not Edward Bromley, Jr. It was a medium-sized room with a single three-quarter bed covered without a crease by a crimson bedspread. The polished hardwood floor was immaculate. There was only one small oriental rug on one side of the bed, a nightstand with a doily, a clock, and an ashtray with no ashes in it. On top of the shiny black chest of drawers there was only a silver comb-and-brush set, carefully arranged, and on the surface of a small writing table there was nothing at all. Three straight-backed chairs and a Morris chair, strategically placed to make the room seem less empty than it was, were the only other furniture, except for a mirror above the bureau and a picture of an English fox hunt on the wall opposite.

That picture plunged Archibald without warning into his childhood. It had hung in the library around the time he first went to nursery school, and in later years, if he had ever been asked about it, he would have replied that he imagined it left the house long before his mother and father. Edward must have found it in the attic. It completed the museum-like effect of his room in which there was not a hair out of place—no pair of slippers under the bed, no crumpled sock on the floor, no opened letter on the writing table. The only thing missing, to complete the effect, was a velvet rope strung between brass poles to keep the public from advancing further.

But he was wrong: there *was* a sign on life. On the

bed, he now noticed, staring at him glassy-eyed, was a large, new, pink-and-brown teddy bear.

"He's mocking me!" Archibald mumbled, and left the room.

ELEVEN

He stood in the hall, rubbing his eyes and looking back and forth at the two doors, one opened, the other closed still. Maybe he should stop now, he thought. Was it worth it to pry like this, to violate so meanly and underhandedly the privacy that had made life for the three of them possible here? So far everything had been so totally, so devastatingly unforeseen. Already with one twist of a doorknob he had discovered something about his brother that he was not at all sure he cared to know. Discovered what? He didn't even know. That's what was really frustrating. He had no idea what Edward's room *meant*.

That decided him. He must see this through to the end. He lunged at Clara's door, grasping the doorknob, and piled with his whole body against the door. It was locked.

Rage rose in this throat. He could taste it. In the next second he was running down the stairs, across the hall, the coatroom, the pantry, into the kitchen. Then, with a bunch of keys from the peg on the wall over the toaster, he ran the same course in reverse, up the stairs two steps at a time, and at last back, breathless and bewildered, before that feminine caprice, that infuriating door. He thrust the keys one after the other into the keyhole, delicately, sensitively twisting and jiggling each, easing it gently in and out, in and out, feeling for the mysteries inside. A key caught, worked profoundly in the innards of the lock, and explosively the door sprung open.

Clara's room was vast, with windows on three walls, and almost the same area as the livingroom on the floor below; and its disorder—perhaps devastation would be a better word—was incredible. A cream-colored rug with a deep soft pile covered the whole floor, wall-to-wall, but was only intermittently visible under the clutter of objects encumbering it. Closest to Archibald was a pile of bedclothes—sheets, pillows, blanket, pink bedspread—on the floor with a tendril of sheet reaching back to the bed, where it was still partly tucked in. The bed itself was king-size—a very Cadillac of a bed—and covered only by a single rumpled sheet upon which were scattered a woman's nightgown, a pair of silk stockings, and a pair of undershorts. A man's undershorts. They were—Archibald could not believe it—dark gray with thick orange stripes in a jagged pattern.

He ignored everything else in the room—the shoes, slippers, stockings and other articles of clothing on the floor everywhere, the piles of clothing on every chair, the chaos of bottles, jars, puffs, tissues on the dressing table and most of the other furniture surfaces—and fixed on that single pair of salamander undershorts. He marched into Edward's room and began opening the drawers of Edward's bureau. Inside each drawer, stuffed to the top, was a Clara-like jumble. (Edward's passion for neatness and simplicity penetrated, apparently, no deeper than visible surfaces.) In the third drawer down, Archibald found what he was looking for: the gray background, the salamander stripes.

He felt dizzy. Everything began to seem a little unreal. To have had this vague, monstrous suspicion, no more than an intuition founded on the most dubious evidence imaginable, was one thing. To have this proof-positive was something else. He ought to have felt exultant at this brilliant, this well-nigh supernatural confirmation of his daring theory: but he was not sure that he felt that way at all. He felt staggered by the enormous burden of revenge that his discovery placed upon him.

Was that burden for real, for keeps? He'd think about that later. For now, here, he'd seen enough. How could a brother and sister who presented such a harmonious image together in public differ so vastly in private? No, it was impossible. Edward's real home, his actual nest, was in that bed with Clara.

He backed out of the room. Fortunately the keys were still hanging in the door and he did not have to try every one in the bunch again: the one that had unlocked locked, and when it had, he worked it off the ring and slipped it into his pocket. Then he thought for a moment and put the key back on the ring. He made doubly certain that nothing was disturbed in Edward's room, closed the door, and returned the keys to the kitchen.

Where to from here? It was scarcely more than midmorning, but he felt a powerful fatigue and a longing for his own room. He climbed the back stairs, pushed his door open, and when he was in his room and had seated himself in his overstuffed chair, he remembered how it had felt, while shopping for trousers at a local department store some weeks ago, to put the old trousers he had been wearing back on after trying on the new ones. The soft *him* quality of the old ones, responding as if from old habit to the exact shape of his thighs and buttocks, was like the feeling of his room around him. The little heaps of books from the library, arranged according to their due dates on the floor, the shelves full of books he had bought. The bed which was made, but not very neatly. The closet door ajar, revealing things messily hung up inside. The mantel, tables, and other surfaces covered with a mild clutter of familiar objects. This was a normal human room!

Normal? His eyes came to rest on a large ball, six inches in diameter on the mantelpiece. It was made entirely of rubberbands. He knew, because he was the maker. Not only that: he had also found all the rubberbands for it, walking about the streets of Sweethill and the metropolitan area.

That ball made him realize to what extent he too was a creature of passions. Not the tiresome, run-of-the-mill bourgeois passions celebrated in movies, TV shows, novels. Money, success, sex. That's where people failed nowadays, he decided. Absolutely no inventiveness in their passions and pastimes. The situation had gotten so bad that a whole branch of the medical profession, psychiatry, and therapeutic technique, psychoanalysis, had been requisitioned to sustain and enforce the general tedium: interesting and unusual passions, like his for causing a truly huge and monumental rubberbandball to arise from the improbable emptiness of suburban streets and sidewalks, were redefined as neurotic systems and "wastes of psychic energy." As though life itself on this ridiculous ball of earth, whirling in a dark and endless universe, were not a waste of psychic energy!

"O, you're such a terrible pessimist!" Clara had said to that, and he had looked up from his bourbon and answered,

"No, I'm not a pessimist. I'm an Archibald."

The rubberbandball, completed almost six months

ago, had been his last grand passion (so named to distinguish it from the passing infatuations that occurred daily and weekly). *Had been.* For now a new one had begun—messier perhaps and lacking the classic simplicity of the rubberbandball—but far more far-reaching in its implications and profounder in its effects—that had to do with bedrooms, ancient suspicion, revenge for a deluded and ruined life, conflagration....

In the public library one afternoon last fall, he had addressed one of his rare questions to the reference librarian, a middle-aged Japanese woman. Her answer had been routine, but on her desk—"What's that?" he could not resist asking.

"This?" she said, holding up a tan spherical object somewhat less than two inches in diameter. "This is a rubberbandball. Haven't you ever seen one? It's a good way to save rubberbands for when you need them."

Archibald had no interest in such a practical use, and he suspected that the woman was deluding herself when she pretended that she did. He couldn't believe that she ever took rubberbands off it once she had put them on: she would be too fascinated with the slow growth of the thing and with the way random additions made its shape become ever more perfectly spherical as it grew. Completely different causes were responsible for the stars and planets being spherical, and different and unrelated causes still were responsible, according to the scientists, for the simplicity of raindrops and the bits of mercury that spill from broken thermometers; but Archibald believed with Euclid, Aristotle, and other ancient Greeks that there was some essential quality in the sphericity shape—something inexpressible in the language of our culture, something mystical, if one enjoyed using that word—that united all these instances. The very scientific principle of simplicity in the explanation of phenomena demanded it.

Despite such interesting speculations, Archibald would probably have quickly forgotten about the rubberbandball, had it not been for one apparently unrelated circumstance: his route home from the library passed by the Sweethill Post Office, in front of which was the usual battery of bright blue mailboxes. And in front of these on his way home, Archibald noticed two rubberbands on the sidewalk. He bent to pick them up. They were the beginning.

He would never have begun had he had to buy the rubberbands. He wasn't that sort of person. It wasn't a matter of parsimony, but of esthetics—the economy of art. To have bought the rubberbands for his rubberbandball would have seemed like winning a tennis match by bribery.

That evening he said to Clara and Edward, "Strange what a difference changing one small sound can make in a word or phrase. For example, think of the difference between a rubberband and a robber band."

They didn't mind him being silly like this. What they didn't realize was that he was expressing his anxiety that a new grand passion had begun and that, by bereaving him of his senses, rubberbands would indeed prove to be robber bands.

Insensibly he began walking more, driving less, and keeping his eyes on the ground when he walked; and at the end of a month of casual gathering, his ball was a full inch in diameter. He was quite pleased with himself until he made some elementary calculations based on the Euclidian theorem that spheres are to one another as the cubes on their diameters.

At that rate a rubberbandball two inches in diameter would take eight months. That was a long time to spend, scanning sidewalks and pavements. And surely he would want a rubberbandball larger than one owned by a mere reference librarian. One three inches in diameter would take 27 months—over two years! But Archibald had already gone further than this. He had already decided that a truly monumental rubberbandball should have a diameter of six inches—a round half foot; and he calculated that the time it would take to gather the substance of such a wondrous object would be eighteen years. That was a little longer than most Egyptologists believed it had taken to build the Great Pyrmaid of Cheops.

The Project appeared doomed. And so it would have been, except for a series of discoveries that Archibald made about the United States Postal Service. Across the street from the Post Office one day not long before Christmas, he found two large rubberbands, and a little further up the street, two more of the same kind. The next day six more were in the same area. This clearly suggested a single person with the rather strange habit of scattering rubberbands as he went. Then a week or two later, after a thaw, he took a new route for his afternoon walk, which led through a low rent housing project a few blocks away and past a number of the special green mailboxes that the Postal Service uses to supply mailmen. In less than an hour he came back with his pockets stuffed with over ninety of the same kind of large dirty rubberbands fished out of the slush.

He was on his way. He found rubberbands of the same kind all over Sweethill—and throughout the metropolitan area—always in connection with the green storage boxes. Evidently a mailman would open the storage box, take out packets of mail deposited there for delivery, and amble up the street, scattering rubberbands that bound the packets as he went. Some mailmen left these rubbery trails, he discovered, and some did not. "Once a scatterer, always a scatterer," he often said to himself, following the path of these unknown slovenly ones. Were they expressing their pent-up feelings of rage and frustration by wasting their employer's property like that? And why were there always—the fact was corroborated again and again—far more rubberbands in poorer than in wealthier neighborhoods? Was there some mysterious and delicate balance between the postman and his environment? Did the mere sight of ugly, squalid surroundings somehow release the negative feelings that manifested themselves in rubberband scattering?

Archibald was thinking that he might like to write a learned paper on this subject someday, when he discovered an even greater bonanza in the parking lot and loading area behind the Sweethill Post Office. He began to prowl there after thaws among the blue and white trucks parked for the night, collecting rubberbands by the fistful. That put him over the top. And there, now, was the huge rubberbandball in its dish on the bureau. Fortunately it attained its planned dimension before the shabby, baggy-trousered trespasser was discovered and asked embarrassing questions.

"Doing? O good sir, I was collecting rubberbands in your parking lot." Impossible! It was too absurd. Too insane.

And now he had a new grand passion—as absurd and as silly, perhaps; and as useless, no doubt. But from this, as seemed likely, there would be more of a consequence: such that the rubberbandball, which shook the house when Archibald bounced it, would roll melting skyward in the flames.

TWELVE

The porch and fenced-in patio of the Contis' house on Foresight Street was aswarm with people. Evidently the neighborhood party was going to be a great success. Even Archibald Bromley was there, separated from his brother and sister, with his back to the porch wall, standing silent and immobile with a drink in his hand, a gray stone in the midst of the living stream.

He wore a necktie and a tweed jacket too wide in the lapels and his thick black curly hair was slicked back in a way that was quite unbecoming. He looked hot and uncomfortable.

And he felt hot and uncomfortable. Why was he standing there? Never mind, he'd go home soon. Only a short walk.

He saw the bony and slender figure of Elsa Robbins nearby and making her way towards him. She was Nora Melby's neighbor and the wife of a drunken dentist by whom she had three children. Archibald liked her because he sensed that she was a kind person with few pretensions, but this did not make him want to speak with her.

"Mr. Bromley..."

"They call me Archibald." He tried to smile.

"Archibald, then. Are you having a good time? It's really an awful crowd, isn't it?"

He felt helpless. She was such a friendly gregarious person and would have been comfortable talking with almost anyone there; but she spoke with him because she thought he needed help. That alone made conversation with her out of the question; but over and above that, her mere residence on Clairmont Street made her part of a world—Edward and Clara's world of lies, he now realized—with which he no longer wished to have any commerce. Maybe she married her husband, too, because she pitied him. The poorest possible reason to get married, thought Archibald—not that he was such a great expert on that particular subject. How could he turn her away without blasting her generosity?

"That's alright," he said. "Look, I'm alright. You mustn't worry about me. I don't talk very much in situations like this, but I like to hear the people talk. So thank you for coming over, but you mustn't worry. I'm perfectly alright."

"O. K. I understand. See you later," she said easily, smiled, and walked off.

He was deeply affected. How few really decent people there were left in the world! He did not include himself in that rapidly shrinking category.

It struck him how precise he had been when he told her he liked to hear people talk. He hadn't said he liked to hear what they were saying. When he stood in one place, a respectful distance tended to develop between him and the people surrounding him, who also had a tendency to turn their backs on that unsettling image of self-contentment and aloofness, Crazy Archie Bromley; and when he moved about, he only got disconnected sentences and sometimes only their middles, ends, or beginnings. That was what he heard now as he moved toward the bar in the patio to have his glass refilled.

"Happiness is what you..."

"... higher and higher every year. It's going to be..."

"... really a lot of fun every time I..."

"But Pat, you know Ralph is in it right up to his..."

As he was about to step through the French doors onto the patio, he glimpsed to the left, by a large potted plant, the backs of Clara and Edward. They were talking with Henry Melby, a short, thin man—a lawyer, Archibald thought—with a little white face, dark-rimmed glasses, and failing hair. That meant Nora Melby must be near. He dreaded meeting Nora. She was new to the neighborhood, to be sure, and gave him no echoes from the past, but she was so brassy, so thin-lipped and gimlet-eyed... He dreaded meeting many people there. Gladys Worthington, for one, would probably appear out of nowhere before long, as she had on the lawn last week. And yet for some reason he did not fully understand, he didn't want to leave just yet. He seemed to be waiting for something—something there for him. He wished he could hide in the darkness somewhere until it appeared.

Or did he only feel the urge to stay because the party was a distraction from the endless round of thoughts and images, picturing the lascivious nights of Edward and Clara? He loathed the way his imagination kept stripping the one of his vest and gold watch chain, the other of her spotless skirt and blouse. It was sickening. It was like rupturing reality itself.

He nudged up to the table where the press of scrubbed and perfumed bodies was the thickest and asked the teenage boy serving drinks—evidently one of the Conti children—for a bourbon and water. It was darker out here, Archibald noted, and a little cooler—though the weather had been so mild for the last two weeks that he had hardly noticed the heat at all. Maybe the darkness would be better. Maybe whatever it was didn't need the light.

Wriggling with his drink out to the relatively free grass again, he became aware of two large evergreens growing along the fence which shut the patio off from the neighbor's lot. They intrigued him. How pleasant it might be, he thought, to slip behind them (there must be space between them and the fence) and stand there in the deeper darkness, sipping his bourbon unmolested. He went to the fence next to them, turned around to the crowd, glanced quickly over all the faces within his view to make sure that no one was aware of him there, and pushed in behind the first tree.

Small branches annoyed his face and larger ones below pulled at his body, but he pressed through to a place between the two trees and the fence, which was relatively free of branches. He was surprised how much he could see from that position, looking out between the two trees into the patio—because from the other side, he remembered, it had looked completely dark between the trees, as though crowded with thick foliage. He checked his clothes. Dark jacket, trousers, tie—and he folded the wide lapels of his jacket inward to cover his white shirt. Then he sipped his drink, feeling relaxed and invisible.

Luckily he didn't smoke. (He'd given up five years ago, not because he wanted to lengthen his life but because he felt challenged by the cigarettes he had to have.) The glowing tip would have betrayed him, and more than likely the dry fronds framing and tickling his face would have caught, and all those spiritual sons and daughters of Moses out in the patio would have been overwhelmed by the sight of Archibald in the Burning Bush....

Not at all a pleasant way to die, he thought. The pilots of the First World War, in the days before parachutes—Guynemer, Fonck, Richthoven, and the rest—had feared going down in flames more than any other fate and more often than not, when caught in that situation, preferred to jump to their certain deaths. Yet this was the death he was planning for Edward and Clara. Wasn't it appropriate to their passion? And it was the death that used to await heretics at the stake, the special doom reserved for those who destroyed the faith that others lived by, tore away the veils of illusion that made us human. They had corrupted the sacred bonds....

He would have to study the matter. Basically the whole cellar, maybe the first floor too, would have to be soaked in gasoline and quickly, before the fumes awakened them, torched. Anything less decisive, less explosive, would almost certainly fall short, because the Sweethill fire station was only three streets—mere seconds—away. One condition made matters much simpler. He would make no effort to conceal the act of arson. This was to be the end of his days as a normal citizen, as well as theirs. For him afterwards, if he did not torch himself as well, there would be only dead meaningless days in a prison, asylum, or whatever. A pity that capital punishment had been discontinued. Suicide, which was temperamentally impossible for many, or getting oneself murdered, which took a lot of courage and ingenuity, were the only ways left to achieve a prompt death.

The disquieting thought struck him that he might just be planning all this *selfishly*, that he might not even care whether Edward and Clara were betraying him by committing incest, that he was only casting desperately about for some means adequately to express the meaninglessness and futility of his own existence. That fireball at the end of his days would express it so precisely, so dramatically, so beautifully....

Perhaps it would be best to lay out large pans of heavier oil on the first floor that would burn at a higher temperature and more fiercely and durably. The first department would not be prepared for a petroleum fire...

"Come over here, Henry!"

"For God's sake, Nora, what's this all about?"

Henry and Nora Melby were less than two feet away, huddling on the other side of the trees.

"I only wanted to tell you, you little jerk, that if you play your cards right and stop trying to be the know-it-all every second of the day and night, you're going to get the whole Jennings account."

"The whole? ... You're crazy, Nora. What gives you...?"

"*Who* gives me... Who, who! Mary-Jean, that's who. She told me Bentley told her it's yours. He knows you've got the brains—I'm glad *he* knows—but he's only a little doubtful about you being too overconfident. Mary-Jean says you ought to try being a little more thoughtful and humble. That's what he likes—humility."

"Nora, baby, you're brilliant, you're beautiful. Humble's the w..."

There were some muffled words that Archibald couldn't catch. They were embracing.

"Upph!" said Nora. "You filthy.... How were the Bromleys—brother and sister—or should I say Mr. and Mrs.?"

"Nora, I swear, I think you are right about them. They behave exactly like some old married couple. Maybe not so old either. I mean the way they cling to each other, practically coo at each other."

"And did you see the other one against the wall, Crazy Archie?"

"Standing there, sweetheart, like a cigarstore Indian, not saying a word to anybody?"

"Weird! Well, at least he didn't have his pants down and his cheeks out, like the other day out on his lawn."

"I bet he jumps right in with old Eddie and Clara when they're at it in the master... "

Nora screamed. Archibald could hear that Nora was screaming. That must be why her husband, Henry, hadn't finished his sentence—that and the fact that he, Archibald, dropping his drink, had crashed through the branches and now stood between them with his back to Nora and facing Henry—or rather, looking down on Henry, who was rather short.

It was strange how distant Nora's scream sounded, considering how close she must have been to him and how long it was going on—much longer, one would have thought, than her lungs would have been able to sustain. Then Archibald realized that time had slowed down and that was why he seemed to be doing everything so slowly and deliberately—as when his right hand, with its fingers extended, moved over the few inches separating him from Henry Melby's fancy sports shirt with a string necktie, gathered together, as it closed into a fist, a considerable bundle of the shirt and the necktie, and lifted this bundle, not at all gently, straight upward, so that the bottom of the shirt pulled completely out of Henry Melby's trousers, the shirt itself ripped as it drew under his armpits, and several buttons popped in various directions like so many grains of popcorn in a popcorn popper.

Archibald had seen this mode of attack used several times in his favorite comic strip, and had always wanted to try it out on someone like Henry Melby.

"Apologize!"

"Apol... For wha... ? You're chokig me!"

"Help! Lights! Get that creep off my husband," Nora yelled. "He's murdering him!" Actually she was a large muscular woman and could have inflicted a considerable amount of damage on Archibald from behind, if it had occurred to her to do so.

Archibald relaxed some of the upward tension on Henry Melby's shirt and rocked him gently back and forth.

"Apologize!"

"For what?" said Henry, growing bolder, sensing the tide of battle beginning to turn, "for words that I said to my wife in private?"

"For expressing disgusting sentiments about my brother and sister. For..."

The patio leapt into brilliant illumination. Somebody had turned on the floodlights; and now, as in the unbelievable vividness of a dream, a semicircular crowd of faces sprang into being, centered on the three figures shining against the dark evergreens.

"Put him down, Bromley!"

"Get that nut out of here!"

"Call the police!"

He recognized some of the voices. It was Elsa Robbins' husband, the dentist, who had referred to him as "a nut." He saw the silhouettes of Edward and Clara in the dimmer light behind, the only guests, apparently, who had remained on the porch.

He could endure the dreamlike, hallucinatory quality of the scene no longer, and he decided, moreover, that it might not be prudent to wait for the apology he had demanded. In fact, the whole idea of an apology had begin to seem a little pointless.

He let go of Henry Melby's shirt with a shove that made its wearer stumble backward but not lose his footing and turned toward the crowd, which melted away to either side of him as he walked to the patio gate and out into the street.

Had he seen Elsa Robbins' face near as he passed by, and were there tears in her eyes, or was that only a part of some other dream? He walked up the middle of the empty street the short distance to his home, and he thought heavily that Clara and Edward would soon follow.

THIRTEEN

"You know, Arch," said George Kaskin, "I think that woman—what's her name?—Nora Melby, might have a bit of a thing for you. I mean, the way she just stood there while you roughed up her obnoxious little husband."

"But she was screaming."

"Well you know, a scream can be ambivalent. You can scream with horror, but you can also scream with pleasure. You know what it's like when a woman screams with pleasure, Arch.... It sounds to me as though she might have been a bit turned on by the whole thing. She certainly doesn't seem that fond of her husband."

"She's as fond of her husband as she is of anybody—except maybe, her dog, Hannibal."

"Well, maybe she has a thing for Hannibal, then." Kaskin expressed his satisfaction with this remark by emitting a nervous, rapidly vibrating laugh that was close to a giggle.

Archibald was annoyed by the way his friend picked out this very minor and trivial detail of his account for comment. Always pleasing himself and getting off onto his own obsessions!

They sat in a small, dirty bar in the neighboring town of Weatherby. Sweethill was dry and Kaskin lived in the city, and Weatherby seemed like a good compromise. Kaskin was a short, heavy-set man with a reddish beard, florid complexion and gray popping eyes—a somewhat improbable member of the English Department of Wenzel College, where Archibald, long before Kaskin's time, had been enrolled for a term after getting out of the army.

"You don't need a college education, Arch. You're living proof that the poor can educate themselves."

Actually Kaskin, who professed to be a Communist, was now more interested in history than he was in English Literature. He also had a somewhat incongruous passion for Greek mythology. He thought of it as expressing the dark chaos out of which mankind, by the slow accumulation of scientific knowledge, had climbed, but it supplied him with a kind of light too. "Every month my wife and my two daughters pounce on my salary, Arch, like the vulture devouring Prometheus' liver, and every month Wenzel renews and deposits it in me all over again."

Archibald scowled at his glass of beer. "It was terrible for them—for Ed and Clara. They didn't say so, they didn't say anything at all when they got home a little after me that night or since, but I know it was terrible for them."

"O I don't know. You pulled a few buttons off a grubby lawyer's fancy shirt. I can't see that's such a big thing to get upset about. Maybe I just don't understand the subtleties. That sort of thing went on all the time where I grew up. People getting drunk.... You know, Arch, if you ask me, they ought to be thankful it wasn't any more than buttons." He spoke in a low, confidential tone, which seemed to suggest that he and

Archibald were in a conspiracy of some kind.

"Nobody was drunk. They said things about my brother and sister that I did not feel I could permit them to say. I demanded that they retract those things. It seemed to me that I was perfectly within my rights in making that demand. But then suddenly everything appeared in a new light. I was the offender, the violator of the peace. Everybody condemned me. Nobody asked what had been said."

"You mean you weren't drunk, Arch, when you decided to go behind those bushes? That was a pretty strange thing to do."

"They weren't bushes. They were trees."

"All right. Trees then. Still...."

"I wasn't drunk. That was only my second drink."

"And before you got there?"

"Stone sober. And what's so strange about going behind a tree?"

"Well, I suppose, if you wanted to take a leak."

"I wanted to be alone."

"At a party? Why did you go to a party if you wanted to be alone? Or if you were at the party and discovered you wanted to be alone, why didn't you go home?"

"I couldn't leave my brother and sister."

"Come off it, Arch. They're adults, now aren't they?"—again the conspiratorial tone—"And you left them there anyway in the end."

"I couldn't help that. And they came home right after me. They didn't say a word. I was sitting in the library...well, I guess they did say a few words. I'm sitting there, when the front door opens and shuts. There's a silence out in the hall, and then a few sad murmurs that I can't catch. And then for some reason they both come into the library at once and switch on the light, and there I am. And it's like they're stunned to find me there. But Ed pulls himself together a little and manages to say, `That's alright, Arch. Don't worry about it. Things like that will happen sometimes.' You know, sometimes I think I really love my brother, if it only weren't for the fact...."

"Fact?"

"But that wakes up Clara, and she has to say something too, and in her insistent analytical way, she wants to know what I'm doing behind those bushes. (She thinks they were bushes too. That's why it bothered me when you called them bushes.) So I say, `Look, Clara, I know you probably won't understand this, but I just had to go in there out of sight. I was copulating with the ghost of Sir Isaac Newton.' And what does she say to that? If you knew Clara at all well, you'd know she blows her bonnet when people say things like that to her. But this time she just looks at me very calmly for a moment, then turns away and walks quietly out of the room. And big brother Eddie mumbles a little something about how that might not have been just exactly the right thing to say at that particular moment. But George, when Clara walked off so quiet like that, it broke my heart."

Kaskin twisted his body impatiently in his side of the booth. "You're getting this out of proportion, Arch. How have things been since? That was four days ago."

"Everything as usual. But strained. Self-conscious. We had a Sunday to get through the next day. But we didn't meet at breakfast and I stayed in my room all day and told them I didn't want dinner. Had snacks. I heard them arguing in their part of the house that night. They hardly ever do that. But since then not a waste word. Only what's necessary. No more. You don't realize what it's like for them. Everybody talks

THE INVESTIGATOR

about everybody else in that neighborhood, especially the old timers like Ed and Clara and me, who've spent their whole lives there. It's their only home. How can they hold their heads up?"

"They have pride, don't they?"

"Their own guilt brought it on."

"What do you mean by that? ...You mean they've lost their self-respect because they feel guilty about something? What about? You know, Arch, your brother Ed doesn't have the air—for me anyway—of Orestes being chased by the Furies. Maybe you're making this whole thing a lot more dark and mysterious than it needs to be. I still haven't gotten a rational explanation from you about what you were doing behind those bushes—I mean, those trees."

"I told you."

"That's right. You wanted to be alone. But that just raises another question: why you felt you had to stay on at the party. And don't tell me it was to be near your brother and sister, in case they needed their diapers changed."

Archibald searched his memory, scowling again at his glass, which was now empty. He remembered his speculations about the best way to transform the house on Clairmont Street in the minimum number of seconds into an unquenchable inferno. But no, he was thinking of those things *after* he went behind the trees— fortunately, because those thoughts were not for Kaskin.

"I'm not sure I can explain this very well," said Archibald, "but when I saw those trees—I have a mind that works like this—when I see something like them, and some new and interesting possibility occurs to me in connection with them— like with the trees the possibility of getting behind them and becoming invisible—then if there is any opportunity to carry the thing out, I simply have to. I've always been like that, as a kid on Halloween, at this boarding school, Queensbury, I went to.... But that wasn't what you asked—and not what I said. I said I wanted to be alone, and you asked why I had to stay at the party when I wanted to be alone. I had to stay at the party because I was waiting for something to happen."

"Well, I guess you weren't disappointed."

Archibald scrutinized Kaskin for a long moment and then said in a careful, measured voice, "I was waiting for something to happen because my brother and sister are committing incest with one another and to the best of my knowledge have been doing so for twenty-four years or more. This is a recent discovery, and I wanted to find out—get some inkling—to what extent, if at all, it was known or suspected in the town. That's what I was waiting for—for some sense of that. So it was very disturbing to hear what the Melbys were saying to each other. My brother and sister are guilty and therefore defenseless. That's why I had to protect them, and that's why I have to destroy them."

FOURTEEN

Kaskin looked away from Archibald and was silent. He looked down at the two glasses on the table, over Archibald's shoulder, toward the front window and the street, then fleetingly at Archibald; and finally he said,

"Would you like another beer?"

Archibald nodded in reply, snorted softly and smiled uneasily. "You can forget what I said—please forget what I said about any intentions—any intentions I might have expressed."

"What intentions? I didn't hear you express any intentions.... But I think you said that this was a recent discovery. May I ask, without being indelicate, how you discovered it?"

"Well, there have been a number of things. First, their general manner and behavior together—the same things the Melbys and, it seems, everyone else have noticed. I even used to joke about it with them. My actual suspicions began when I started to think about some very early memories, intuitions. That's difficult to explain. It goes into the dark past, irrationalities, myths—what you think of as the age of ignorance and superstition and I sometimes think must have been a time of godlike intuition and harmony with the universe."

"Yes," Kaskin said with his strange giggly laugh, "you and I have had more than one difference of opinion on that question. But I hope you don't base your condemnation of them on your 'godlike intuition.' I can't really say that I'm that fond of Clara after that little run-in we had in your house last year...."

"She's really sensitive on those matters of religion."

"But I think she would be within her rights—she and your brother Ed—in insisting that you be on pretty firm ground before you condemned them go whatever you are thinking of."

"I'm not thinking of anything. Remember?"

"O right. But as I say, not feeling particularly welcome in your house, I don't feel that fond of them—especially Clara—so I wouldn't like to find myself in the role of the God Apollo, flying down from the heavens to cast my decisive vote for their innocence."

"No, I've got the goods on them."

"Or 'the bads' would maybe be a better expression.

You've seen them—caught them—actually going at it?.

"No, not that. As good as.... A little over a week ago, I went up to their bedrooms. They're in their own part of the house, I in mine. We're almost completely private from one another—or rather, they from me and I from them."

"And when you think of all the people in the world who don't even have a mud hut."

"Maybe we'd have been better off in a mud hut."

"If you *were* in one, I don't think you'd say that."

"So I went into their part, where I haven't been in years, and looked into their bedrooms. And there was a pair of his underpants in her bed."

"O wow! But was that the only thing?"

"That's the main thing. His room looks very unlived-in. But isn't that enough?"

"Well, Arch, when the evidence is circumstantial like that, there's always the possibility that some other construction, some other interpretation, can be put on the facts than the obvious one."

"Like what, for example?"

"Well, you're sure they are his underpants and that they don't belong to the ice man or the milkman or the oil delivery man or the paperboy...."

"Impossible. I'm home all day and she's out, and there are other pairs of exactly the same very unusual design—remarkably like the design on your salamanders—in his bureau drawer."

"Alright, then, they're his. But then you have to consider the spirit with which they may have been removed from the person—the various ways they may have got there. Is there a laundry hamper around there? There must be."

"In the bathroom, I think."

"Good. Common territory. Maybe she fished them out of the laundry hamper and took them to bed with her because she wanted to smell them. It may not be a very praiseworthy habit, but it certainly isn't criminal for a woman to enjoy smelling a man's underpants, even if they happen to belong to her brother."

"George—somehow it just doesn't sound like Clara."

"O, I don't know. Of course, I don't know her as well as you do. But I can picture...."

Archibald gathered from the glitter in Kaskin's eyes that he was enjoying the picture.

"The point is, Arch, you're just never going to be absolutely sure about this unless you actually catch them in the act—*in flagrante delicto*, as they say—a phrase I've always enjoyed because it sounds as though it might mean 'in their flaming delectabilities,' or 'their hot delights.'"

"Look, George, this is a serious matter for me. Lives might be at stake. I'm beginning to regret that I told you anything about it." He wanted to add that Kaskin seemed completely lacking in human feeling, but he decided that was maybe too extreme.

"Sorry, Arch. I guess maybe I'm a little irrepressible sometimes. What I don't understand, though, is—if they are guilty of the act, as you say—then how can you blame Henry Melby for suspecting it? And also, what's so terrible about a little quiet, friendly incest in these liberated times? But if they have to be punished for their acts, as you seem to think—again, how can you blame the Melbys for spreading the word and relieving you of the burden of punishment?"

Archibald felt impatient. "The answer to all that is simple. It's a family matter. The Melby's are out of it. I can speak of the guilt of my brother and sister. The Melbys can't. They have no right. I am the only one aggrieved and therefore the only one entitled to punish."

"That's primitive! That view went out with the forerunners of Aeschylus."

"It's come back."

"And as in the vendetta system, you'll punish them without even making sure of their guilt."

"I'll make sure. I'll catch them in the act."

"And they'll catch you in the act of catching them." Kaskin giggled. "That'll make a pretty scene."

"No, I'll observe them without them observing me. I've figured out a way."

"Just as you figured out a way at the party to observe without being observed!"

"I'm generally pretty good at inventions and devices. I think I've given you some instances of that."

"Yes, I'm sure you are—when your heart is in it. But this one may be too big, too complicated for you, even you. Not everybody can step into the armor of Achilles. There's something about this that's overwhelming you, keeping you from doing your best, sapping your strength. Give it a rest, Arch! Forget one of your obsessions for once. Forget yourself. Look at other people. See what kind of obsessions they have. It s quite a picture they make. A real tableau. You ought to let me take you some places. Magical places. You're too tied to that house. And Clara—tied to Clara. Get out of it. Then maybe you'll find that you don't really care all that much what's going on—or not going on—in it. There's so much suffering, so much injustice in the world that you don't know anything about. You'd be shocked. You'd forget your little problems. I'd like to take you to visit some American Indian friends of mine. The forgotten people."

"The pure products of America...."

"Right, Arch, a lot purer than any of us."

"The pure products of America go crazy."

"They sure do. Or at least they are driven crazy, and you can't blame them."

"A Hell of an English Teacher you are, Kaskin! That's a famous line of poetry, and you're misinterpreting it."

"Right. William Carlos Williams. So who cares? Poetry means whatever you're inspired to think it means. I didn't know you were into poetry."

"I'm not."

"So why don't you go with me to Sybil Maypole's poetry reading tomorrow night? I think you'd enjoy her. She's really good. Very lively. Very unusual effects. She's getting quite a large following. In fact, it might be a squeeze. getting in. It's at the Thin Gravy Gallery, and when you try getting more than twenty or thirty people into that place, the walls start groaning and sweating. What do you say?"

"I don't know...."

"You don't know. I don't know either, Arch. I think you're going to turn into a little old lady if you're not careful. You're a perceptive guy, but you've spent twenty-four years—the best third of your life—doing exactly the same thing, the same nothing, day after day. How do you stand it? Day after day, putting more rubberbands on the same old rubberbandball...."

"The rubberbandball's finished. I told you."

"...until you start dreaming of monstrous crimes and monstrous punishments for maybe innocent people. With all your advantages, you could do so much—still. Haven't you ever wanted to break out? Just *break out* and start over?"

"O.K. I'll go with you tomorrow night."

FIFTEEN

This is ridiculous, Archibald thought, as he backed his Volkswagen into a space on a steep incline leading up from Kaskin's house, a large two-family in a street of two-families. A workers' street to all appearances. Yet two or three blocks away the houses were expensive and grand—very academic posh. Ridiculous. He probably wasn't even dressed right for a place like Thin Gravy Gallery. He wore a clean work shirt and a pair of greenish worker's trousers. He should have worn jeans. He didn't own any jeans.

He felt the sharp edges of a newly-made key in his pocket and thought of Edward and Clara and the surprise on their faces—particularly Clara's—when he announced that he was going out without dinner for the evening.

"I had something to eat a little while ago."

Feeling the key in his pocket as he said that. Without a drink either.

"I'll have one at Kaskin's. Or if not, I'll survive." That reply had a barb in it. Edward probably wouldn't have survived, and maybe not Clara either. He was feeling better, more triumphant, than he had since the fiasco at the Contis'. That he was going out may have had something to do with it, but not much. The going out was ridiculous. It was the key.

Perhaps realizing that they would need some respite from Archibald, Edward and Clara had decided a week ago to go through with the vacation idea and had driven to the Cape the previous Saturday to look at a cottage that had been advertised. They had accepted by phone, sent a deposit, and the key with a note from the landlord had arrived in yesterday's mail. This morning, the key, note, and torn envelope still lay on the little table in the hall, and Archibald had the key duplicated at the local hardware store. That was the key in his pocket. The new plan was underway.

Kaskin let him in and led him to a small sitting room with an upright piano and on the wall a large bad charcoal drawing of a nude woman. In the opposite corner on a table was the wire cage where the salamanders rustled from time to time. Archibald had no desire to see them again.

"Let me fix you a little something, and then we'll be off."

Archibald heard voices in another room. He had met Kaskin's wife so briefly that he could not clearly remember what she looked like. Did Kaskin even have a wife? Maybe he copulated with the ghost of Helen of Troy or consorted with the vulture that devoured the liver of Prometheus. But didn't he have daughters? Why so he said. But so did the King of the Elves.

"What's this?" said Archibald, looking down into the dark contents of a red and yellow ceramic cup, then up into the popping eyes and wild red beard and hair near him on the couch.

"The elixir of the gods. Drink and give thanks to George Kaskin, compounder of Devilish potables."

Archibald sipped. Not bad. Faintly acrid, but dry and smooth. He looked at Kaskin again, thought of the salamanders in their cage, and taking sudden resolve, drained the cup in several large gulps.

"That's the brave boy!" said Kaskin. "I knew he had courage the first time I saw him clip his ripcord onto the wire in that lumbering old Gooney Bird. Shall we jump?"

"Let's jump," said Archibald, as they both got up from the couch, "onto Sybil's Maypole."

"You'll wish, before the evening is over, that Sybil would jump onto your Maypole."

"Is that her real name?"

"Nah. Everything about Sybil is fictional."

They walked to the Square and took the subway, and when they arrived, Thin Gravy was already getting full. It was a long, very narrow room plunging deep into the building from the street. Books and benches lined the walls; and there were other benches at right angles to these in short ranks before the poet's lectern, which was not much more than halfway into the room. Beyond this there were posters, an easel, two broken chairs, a pay telephone. At the very far end of the room was a rolltop desk almost buried under a mass of papers and books.

"She's professional, at least," murmured Kaskin when they had settled on a bench. "Some of the people that Jake lets in here don't know the first thing, and you can get some really drippy performances. Jake's amateur hour. Walking embarrassments."

Without warning the lights went out, and at the same time someone slammed the door to the street. That was a good thing because the place—the little honeycomb of backless benches—was already packed. Body pressed on body. It was going to be a hot evening.

Slowly light began to be recreated—lavender and blue—emerging from several revolving fixtures along the walls.

"Those are hers," whispered Kaskin. "I've never seen them before."

A faint sound of static became audible, warning those who were aware of it that a sound system had been turned on, and shortly thereafter an enormous belch, many times longer and louder than life, rolled and gurgled from the middle air beyond the lectern. There were some titters in the audience at this, but the prevailing mood was respectful silence. Archibald, who was ready to burst, found this audience reaction hard to believe.

The sound system farted—the fart, like the belch, huger than life. It's as though the whole room, thought Archibald, removed to another world, had been shoved up a giant's asshole. After the fart came the sound of piddle falling into a toilet—male piddle. That sound in itself was ambiguous, of course. It could have been many things, since many things sound like that: mountain springs falling into hillside basins, leaks in basements, kitchen taps left dribbling into gradually filling sinks, the last of the lemonade being poured on hot August evenings; but the conclusion that it was piddle was immediate because of its association with the preceding sound. Archibald noticed this because he had become interested lately in the surprising extent to which most of what we think we observe turns out, on examination, to be pure interpretation, empty imagination, mad hallucination.

In the strange flickering light a humanoid shape was dimly visible at the lectern, and from that direction a deep female voice intoned:

> I am the Breaker of the Wind,
> saith the Lord, for all who've sinned
> the Savior and Redeemer.
> I am the Holy Streamer.

Light, evidently from a spotlight somewhere, shone weakly at first, then with ever increasing intensity, on the green sequinned dress, leathery face, dark hair, and glittering black eyes of a plump middle-aged woman with deeply crimsoned lips. Her dress had long sleeves, green and glittering, and she wore enormous gold and glass earrings. Her right arm was heavily braceleted and her left was plunged into the body of an almost unbelievably ugly hand puppet.

It had the face of a doll, blond, pink, and fat-cheeked, and the body of a serpent, whose tail hung green, limp, and threadbare along the sequinned arm which impaled it. Archibald marveled that a doll with a face so wizened and pouting and so distorted by some strange agony should have been manufactured—not at first, obviously, with that reptilian body. At the line,

>I am the Holy Streamer,

it seemed to stand, looking down at an imaginary penis, which it held in its three-fingered hands.

In the full light now, she looked at the audience—the woman, not the puppet—and said, "The first group of poems I am going to read, I call 'Twingies'—a new form of my own invention. A Twingy—or a Twingey: it may be pronounced either way, with the *g* hard as in 'thing' or soft as in 'tinge'—a Twingy is a poem of moderate length in free-flowing rhythms, whose purpose is to awaken the buried feelings of guilt and violence which are in all of us...."

"Excuse me!" said Archibald. He knew as soon as his voice sounded that he had made a mistake and that his contribution would not be welcome, but there was no stopping in mid-swing. "Excuse me. You speak of awakening buried feelings. Wouldn't the buried feelings have to be dug up? There wouldn't be any point in awakening them if they were buried. Conversely, if they are the sort of feelings that can be awakened, perhaps they are not buried at all, but only asleep."

Some of the people on the benches ahead had twisted the upper halves of their bodies around and were looking furiously at him, and he felt sure that he could feel many more such glances from behind, where no such twisting would be necessary to administer them, delicately penetrating him like so many acupuncture needles, or perhaps like the needles one sticks into a Voodoo doll.

"Quite right," said Sybil, "I always marvel at the perspicacity—to say nothing of the perspicuity—of my audiences. And therefore, good sir, I have chosen the first poem especially for you. It's entitled, 'The Bare Bottomed Buffoon.'" To the accompaniment of titters in the audience, she rolled her eyes upwards and threw her head back while her puppet danced gaily about with its tail flopping, clapping its maimed hands and looking up in agonized expectation, like a perverse dog, waiting to be whipped. Then while she chanted her poem, punctuated by various booms, squeaks and gurgles from the sound system, the puppet danced to the rhythm of the words and clarified its images with a variety of obscene gestures.

> Rage, rage, fill up the spillholes of atrocity!
> Let Nora catch his buttocks bare,
> where Hannibal and all the elephants
> shall bark the angry cunctor,
> lurking, out, burning, from his bush!
>
> I Sybil sing
> siblings syllabent in their ecobodies' ecstacy,
>   eco echo ego
> while hanging from the rafter the long dark
>   brother
>   ringing the churchbells in his billies
>   chirping the conflagration of his Eva
>   crowing old Daddy-Adam to his doom

> Her pseudo-belly heaved
>   PING PING
> went the   tendrils
> Sheet shambles, Ah, the sad-shucked
>   Salamander!
>
> O but that scrofulous one tossed victims to his
>   fire—
>   revolting his revolt!
>   that left him strumming silly dildos of
>   despair,
> festooned, frumpish, with last night's fuck.

With the last line, Sybil and the puppet drilled nearly parallel looks at Archibald from their slightly different directions. There was no choice. He obviously had to reply. Ignoring the puppet and looking fixedly at Sybil, he stood up in front of his seat, which was on the aisle, stepped into the aisle, and waited while Kaskin, giggling softly, followed. Then in the second or two that Archibald's eyes and Sybil's remained locked, what he had known would happen happened, and the ghost of Burlingame, bearing yet another version of Hickory Dickory Dock, entered his mind and mouth, and the two of them, ghost and living man, intoned in a clear, curiously nasal voice:

> Slippery, slobbery, slock.
> The cunt went round the cock.
> The cunt came off.
> The cock came out.
> Slippery, slobbery, slock.

He pulled his eyes from Sybil, threaded his way the few steps down the aisle to the door, opened it and, passing into the street, left it open for Kaskin to close after them.

SIXTEEN

"Well done, Arch," said Kaskin as the Thin Gravy Gallery receded behind them. "A couple more *coups* like that and you'll be well-known in the local literary community."

"I don't want to be well-known in the local literary community.... That was all very strange.... Kaskin, I think you have some explaining to do."

"Wha...t? What does that threatening tone signify? What have I done?"

"You know best."

"Now come off it! It seemed to me that everything that went on was thoroughly ordinary and uncomplicated. This dame comes out—excuse me; the feminists don't like us to use that word—this slut comes out and puts on a really weird show, and you slip it to her right in the middle of her following—and very deftly too, if I may say so, for an unemployed mathematician and rubberband collector. So what could you possibly be grumbling about?"

"That poem she read, that she said was especially for me, was full of references to my problem—to the things I told you about yesterday."

"References? I didn't hear any references."

"The salamander. The salamander underpants that my brother left in my sister's bed—'sheet shambles' was one phrase I think she used."

"Arch, you've got to be kidding. Your brother's underpants weren't in that poem."

"No? Then what about Nora and her dog Hannibal barking, and siblings making love with the dark brother—myself presumably—hanging in the rafters watching?"

"I don't believe this. There *was* something in it about

Hannibal, the Carthaginian general in the First Century, B.C., and the Roman general, Fabius Cunctor, who opposed him."

"George."

"What?"

"What did you put in that drink I had at your place?"

Kaskin giggled. "Arch, I swear, there was nothing in that cup but a touch of sugar and lemon peel and a little vegetable coloring. There was nothing in it but that and your suspicion and your imagination. But I will admit, they may make the strongest drink of all."

"Alright, then those things I heard in the poem—obviously I'm not able to quote them exactly—actually were in the poem. All those things coming together like that is just too much of a coincidence. George, you wrote that poem yourself, based on what you know about me, when you knew I was coming to the reading, and you gave it to your friend Sybil this afternoon to put me on this evening."

"Arch, I swear I didn't do that. Look, you brought it all on yourself when you interrupted her with that comment before she even began to read."

"It would have happened some other way. If she hadn't said that about the poem being for me and had just read it without any previous contact between us, with me just sitting there in the audience, there would have been no way for me to reply, and it would have been even more devastating than it was. Actually I mucked up your neat little trick by interrupting like that."

"Look, Arch, I swear—what more can I do?—I swear by all that's holy...no, I don't believe anything is holy. I swear on my honor as a human being that I didn't do it."

"Maybe you're not a human being."

"Well, if I'm not a human being, then I must be some kind of devil, right? Then in that case—I believe this is the way devils are supposed to function—I would have accomplished my aim, not by writing Sybil's poem for her, but more simply by just giving you the appropriate hallucination. So either way—devil or human—I didn't write it."

"Unless, of course, you're just an ordinary liar and don't mind being foresworn."

"Yes, of course, that *is* possible. Aren't you brilliant to see that possibility! But it might be more fruitful for you to consider how much of this you may simply be manufacturing—how much of it may be sprouting a little too luxuriantly out of the fertility of your own imagination. Maybe you need help, Arch."

"O I'm sure I do. But I can't say the thought distresses me. You know, if you *were* trying to drive me insane by presenting me with trumped-up evidence of my own insanity, you wouldn't succeed because I don't really care whether I'm insane or not. The word may be meaningless. We may be living in an insane world."

"Bravado. I hear a tone of bravado."

"I'm sure you're right about that too.... Where are we going?"

"To Jim Balam's house. There's a party going on there tonight. You'll enjoy it."

They walked several blocks in silence, and once again they were among two-family houses and seemed to have entered a workers' neighborhood—though this one was unfamiliar to Archibald. He felt loose boards under his shoes as they went up a short flight of steps and rang a doorbell. As they waited in the semi-darkness of the porch, where he could see what appeared to be the remains of a broken rocking horse in one corner, a sense of absurdity, almost of panic, swept through him. Why had he so thoughtlessly, so uncritically placed himself under the guidance—if not actually in the power—of this sinister improbable person? Sinister? O Arch, he said to himself, observing Kaskin's short figure in the shadows—the thick bare legs in old army shoes, the bottom fringe of his jean shorts, his white eyeballs in the dark—O Arch, he's not sinister. He's ridiculous. He's nothing!

The front door opened, splashed him with light, and Kaskin seemed to spring into existence. His legs were red, and under his striped tee shirt with its vee neck, his chest was broad and hairy.

"George!" said a deep voice. The man was tall with curly black hair, a huge nose, and dark-rimmed glasses. "I should have known it was you. Timed to the min..."

"JIM!" Kaskin said suddenly and very loudly. Then, lowering his voice, he added in his best confidential manner. "Jim Balam, I'd like you to meet my friend, Arch Bromley."

"Pleased to meet you, Arch." Balam's hand felt huge in Archibald's and potentially very powerful, but it was soft, flaccid, and unused to labor, or even to handling the things of this world. There was a murmur of voices inside, and somebody's finger picked out a few notes on a piano.

"Who's here?" said Kaskin. "Timothy, Patrick, Cynthia, Steven...I'd like Arch to meet them all, before he goes on with a piece of business that he has begun to find very absorbing."

"O yes, all here, all here and more!" Balam's large voice seemed to match his hands.

"Jim, you're not a musician by any chance, are you?"

Archibald asked as they went through a dark corridor toward the light.

"Why yes. Horn player. And I do a little conducting. What drew you to that conclusion?"

"Your hands."

"My hands?"

"Well, yes, and the piano. Your hands have a quality.... They must be exquisitely cared-for."

"They have to be...." A door opened, and they entered the glare. "Here, everybody..." A dozen or fifteen people in the room sat in various positions on the floor or on couches and chairs, with glasses of wine (there were carafes here and there) and plates of food. "Here, everybody, is Arch, Arch...."

"Bromley," said Archibald.

"Arch Bromley fresh from Sybil Maypole. And you all know this vile little cur," Balam continued. Kaskin giggled.

"Here, Arch, sit down on this empty chair between the Jordans, a married couple who made the mistake of sitting near to one another. We expect them to start tearing each other to pieces any moment now. We want you to have an exciting time."

"Jim's sense of humor can be really disgusting sometimes," said the woman. "That's Timothy and I'm Patrick."

She was plump and vigorous, and her breasts swung crazily in her tee shirt as she reached over to shake hands. Large green eyes glittered up through a strand of blond hair into his. Her mouth was wide and friendly.

"Patrick, he might not be interested in sex," drawled Timothy in a high thin voice with his head slanted at an odd angle.

"You can gather from those two introductory remarks the level we are on around here," she said. Her hips, thighs, and crotch filled her jeans to bursting. "But we have some nice times."

Somehow none of this surprised Archibald. He felt as though he had returned to an earlier stage of his existence, one in which he had been more at home.

"Patrick?" he said. "That's your..."

"Yes, it *does* sound a little strange, doesn't it? I mean, when you look at me carefully."

"A great deal of care is not required," said Timothy.

"I was christened Patricia, and that got shortened to Pat. Then Timothy and I, in the only original move in the whole process, lengthened it to Patrick. You see, he's always been a bit of a fruit, and that kept him performing for a year or two longer than he would have otherwise. Would you like to meet Carlos?"

"Couldn't we possibly just stow Carlos for the moment?" said Timothy.

"Why yes, dear, if he makes you feel uncomfortable, certainly. I only thought that, since Arch here evidently has a little pizazz of his own, he might enjoy the company of another male who has what it takes."

Timothy's slender, apparently boneless body was draped over a low chair which was itself merely a piece of canvas hung on an iron frame. His face, faintly triangular, had sensitive features—soft ladylike eyes, clear, dark eyebrows, and sensuous lips. He uncoiled his body ever so slightly and explained,

"Carlos is a bull fighter that Patricia met in Mexico City last winter. He's been our houseguest now for three months, and you might find him a little dull because he still doesn't speak a word of English. In the communication that he and Patrick conduct with one another daily and nightly, he doesn't need any English and she doesn't need any Spanish."

"Timothy darling, are you still having your affair with that wizened little secretary of yours?"

In the general din and murmur of the party, Archibald didn't stay tuned for Timothy's answer; something totally absorbing, not far away, had caught his attention.

SEVENTEEN

"Never, never, never!" Patrick's brassy, educated voice broke in on his consciousness. What was she talking about? What had the conversation moved to while he sat oblivious of it, contemplating that face, toward which he was now moving, stepping carefully among arms, legs, torsos.

"May I sit down?"

"Of course."

"What's she saying 'Never, never' about?"

"She's saying it ought never be permissible for one human being to kill another. That's what everybody's been talking about."

Her voice explaining these things to him, Archibald thought, was like her face turned toward him. It sounded level, matter-of-fact, almost flat, and yet, somehow mixed with that, was a suggestion of softness, of dream, of something unexplained. As for her face, many would have considered it plain. It was oval, pale and faintly freckled. Quiet slate-gray eyes. A friendly mouth, wide, calm. Yes, thought Archibald, the incredible calm, the stillness that seemed to come from her.... Her very nondescript quality—her hair, for example, not blond, not brown, not really to be described at all, unless one were to insist that it was colorless—all contributed to that calm which seemed to bring him to rest in a way that he had not been at rest for a quarter of a century.

"What do you think about that?" he asked.

"About the question of killing? She's right, of course. I agree with Patrick."

"I'm not sure I do."

She sat upright on one side of a large ottoman, with room on it for two, that had been pushed against a wall. Her feet, in sneakers, crossed one another where they rested on the rug, and her hands were lightly folded in her lap. Her spine was straight but relaxed. It seemed as though she might sit there without moving for hours.

Archibald sprawled, a little too large for his perch, sometimes lunging forward to listen, chin in hand, and sometimes lounging back against the wall, even drawing his knees up under his chin, which tended to draw his trousers down over his buttocks.

Archibald Barasol.

"What about Hitler?" he called out to the group, and in the momentary silence that name created, added, "who killed millions? Wouldn't it have been right to kill him?"

Archibald suddenly felt as though he had just arrived at Queensbury and was proving himself in his first class.

"No, Arch," said Patrick, "it wouldn't have been right. Killing him would not bring back one life, not one single life, of all those millions. It would only be doing to him as he did to others. It would be doing things in his way, accepting his style, his values. It was a pity that he managed to kill himself. That was his final crime."

"Alright then," said Archibald, feeling exquisitely sharpened in these new surroundings, "suppose someone, or some group of people, by the mere fact and manner of their existence, have caused—no, excuse me—are causing the slow, inevitable physical and spiritual death of another, or of others. Isn't it within his, within their right—their duty even, and function as a form of life, to destroy what's destroying them?"

"I can't answer that, put in general terms like that," she replied. "Are you sure there *is* such an instance? Can you give me a specific example?"

Archibald squirmed, and as he shifted his position on the ottoman, he could feel his pants being pulled down. He was baring himself in public. He couldn't help it. It was as though, not he, not anything he was willing or desiring, was doing it, but that his environment itself was doing it. His surroundings were doing it. The ottoman was doing it. Or someone—where had Kaskin gone?—someone who had made up and put on all these things for his delusion and benefit and so was acting through them, was doing it.

"Well," he said, "I guess you've put me on the spot.... Well, let me pose the case, say, of a younger brother, living with his older brother and sister. The mother and father were dead. It was the family house. He had come back from the army, the war. For some funny reason, he had never gone to college, even though a lot of people said he had talents. He kept playing pranks on people, getting himself in trouble, getting himself expelled, using his intelligence on futile aimless things like that, amusements—because—no one knew this, but it was true—because his elder brother pretended to admire him for it, admired his exploits and egged him on...because, you see, the older brother had a guilty passion for the sister, who was a lot younger than he was, but only a year or two older than the younger brother.... The mother had died and the father was in poor health and all the elder brother wanted to do in his whole life was live in the house with his sister, making love to his sister.... And that's where they are and that's what they are doing when the younger brother comes back from the army. So they decide to take him in and look after him, as they put it, because he's had a bad time in the army and the war and because that will put a good face on their living together, brother and sister. And so they let him live in the servant's room, and everyone in the town thinks they have sacrificed themselves, not getting married, either one of them, so that they can look after him, helpless little brother, when in reality it's all so they can be illicitly married to each other, going at it together, night after night in the big master bedroom, while he lies alone in the servant's room, beating his meat, with no one but the memory of his friend, who was killed in the army. But you see—now here's the real point—they, the brother and sister really put it on him that he is helpless all these years. They cultivate his illness, his strangeness, for their own purposes, as I described, until finally they've destroyed him. Or rather, even though he is not yet completely destroyed and still has just enough life left in him to retaliate, if he can bring himself to do it, that's the only thing he can do, because from old habit they still have this tremendous psychic authority over him. They are still—in a sense, they are still manufacturing his reality for him and deluding him with it. The only way he can possibly escape from this slow death they have gotten up for him is to pull it all down at once by destroying them, burning them, purging his life at last."

He glanced around from where he stood. He did

not remember getting up. The whole room was silent, looking at him, even though this had been only one of many conversations going on at the same time when he started. In a far corner he could see the shadowy figures of Kaskin and Jim Balam, the host, standing with a third man. He became aware of cold air on his buttocks and pulled up his pants.

"I'm sure there are many similar kinds of situation," he continued, "that one might imagine or describe or experience. But maybe this one will serve. The point is, that the person in the example can get free, can come to life, only by killing others. There is absolutely no other way. And I would maintain that there is a law of life that applies to men every bit as much as to jaguars and that says that the destruction, the killing, is necessary to life and therefore justified."

Patrick had her mouth—her large sensuous mouth with its thick lips and prominent teeth—open to reply; but the woman with whom Archibald had been sitting on the ottoman had stood up, and her slate-gray eyes, usually so calm, were wide and white with anger, and in her even, quiet voice she said,

"Your law—your law of survival and preservation and the right to violence—applies to *men*, I notice, to *men* and jaguars—not to *women*, O no! Women and what? Sheep, lambs, cows? All those scheduled to be swallowed up in your holy law of violence. Will there be no end to this chauvinism?" Her voice, though quiet, was as cold and hard as the polished round pebbles that one pours in among meshing gears in order that they may grind to a halt.

"Cynthia, that's not the crucial point, dear," said Patrick. "The question overtly proposed by the story, of course, is whether the younger brother is justified in killing his older brother and sister—punishing them, or rather killing them in a kind of self-defense. Now the point that we generally make when the question of self-defense is raised is that there is always some better way to handle it. Don't shoot the burglar who's broken into your house, call the police—et cetera. But that solution has been rendered somewhat questionable in this instance by the real or imagined psychological complexity that Mr. Bromley—that Arch—has woven into it. I would like to suggest that all that has to be sorted out first and that the young man in the story"—her large eyes opened wide and looked directly at Archibald—"is in really deep psychological trouble. Obviously the solution, purely in terms of action, of the dilemma posed by the story is for the young man simply to walk out. But that, as Arch indicates, is impossible from a psychological standpoint. So the clear answer is that he needs clinical help. His resort should be to the services of a good psychiatrist rather than to guns, sticks of dynamite, drums of gasoline, or what not."

The room was beginning to stir, and one sensed that the collective attention, having been briefly focused on Archibald and the question he raised, was about to scatter again into its several directions. All that remained to accomplish this transformation smoothly and gracefully was for Patrick to say something that signified a shift from public concern to private.

"But Arch, come on over here and let's you and I talk about this a little more."

EIGHTEEN

"You haven't eaten or drunk a thing since you came," said Patrick when he had arrived at his old straight-

THE INVESTIGATOR 109

backed chair beside her. "There are still some goodies over on the buffet. Help yourself." Archibald returned with chicken, potato salad, and wine. "You know," he said, settling, "I really admire your intellect. I don't agree—not completely anyway, and maybe not at all—but you've already clarified a lot of things for me."

He was a little mortified to hear himself tacitly acknowledging that the general problem he had posed was in fact his own, but what harm could there be, he thought, in owning up to the obvious?

"Thank you," she said, "I think we were all carried away somewhat by your story. Very sweeping. Passionate even."

"Yes," said Timothy's high voice, and when Archibald turned around, there he was with his head cocked to one side. "You were so involved with it, anyone could see it was about someone you knew well—maybe even intimately. How did it turn out? Did the guy really do in his horny siblings?"

"I'd be willing to wager," said Patrick with a smile at Archibald, "that the story hasn't reached its conclusion yet."

"No, but it will have to soon," said Archibald. Timothy yawned, uncoiled his body from his canvas chair, and stood, seeming to undulate gently over them. "I'm going to look for more chicken and wine. I'll try not to get lost, but meanwhile if the house goes up in smoke or the naughty siblings simmer in a cauldron, give me a whistle, so I can come back and watch." And he sauntered off.

"He has a tremendous appetite," said Patrick, "and eats fantastic quantities. You wouldn't believe it, the way he stays thin like that and seems so lackadaisical. I have a weight problem and have to watch what

I eat. Not him. You'd never guess it, looking at him, but he has a huge metabolism and burns vast amounts of energy. That stuff I was saying before about him being a fruit and not having what it takes was a lot of crap. He was marvelous while it lasted. And his secretary is beautiful. Actually I'm jealous as Hell."

Archibald thought it might be indelicate at this point to inquire about the consolations provided by Carlos, the bullfighter, and anyway he had more pressing matters on his mind, so he remained silent, and she went on.

"But you and I have to say something more about your story—about the story you told."

"Yes, well, it seems to me that your solution may be a little oversimplified. You define things in a certain way and then the solution seems obvious; but in fact your definitions have distorted the situation with a lot of interpretation. So there are these two worlds: the world of the interpretation and of the actual situation, and the solution, the suggested action, works beautifully in the world of interpretation, but in the actual situation it accomplishes nothing because the two worlds have so little to do with each other."

"Can you give me an example? What distorting interpretation?"

"Well, according to your interpretation, there is this psychological part that is somehow separate—separable—from the actual facts. If you assume that—define things that way—then the solution becomes easy. You send the guy to a psychiatrist, who takes out his magical psychiatric whiskbroom and sweeps away all those nasty psychological cobwebs, and then it just becomes a clear factual problem that we can all understand, including the guy himself, who is now thinking clearly like the rest of us. And then, as you say, he just simply walks out without harming anybody."

"Well, what's wrong with that?"

"Only one thing."

"What thing?"

"The guy that comes out of the psychiatrist's office 'cured' is not the same guy that went in. The guy that went in was permitting himself to be transformed, that is, he was letting himself be killed. He wasn't struggling to survive, as I maintain it's the nature of life to do."

"Bullshit. You're splitting hairs. A man walked in. A man walked out. Nobody was killed."

"That's looking at it from one side, from the observer's frame of reference, as they say in the Theory of Relativity. And that's a true observation—but only for that observer in his world of interpretations, his distortions, his prejudices. You're O.K., you're on safe ground when you only claim it's a true observation for him—for that observer only. But when you insist that it's absolute and applies everywhere universally, then you get into a lot of trouble."

"What trouble?"

"Trouble with the man himself, the patient, and with his frame of reference."

"I just don't see it. What's so glorious about his frame of reference?"

"It's not that it's glorious. It's just there. It's indestructible as part of the total picture. The way he sees it in his frame is every bit as true—as partially true, which is the only kind of truth possible—as the way you see it in yours. For him, the death he would suffer in the psychiatrist's office is as real, as actual, as the death he would suffer by remaining in the house—or by cutting his own throat. To say that he will remain alive simply because the same pair of legs will be walking around afterward is an unworthy definition of human life—so it seems to me in my frame. And in his frame it's utterly ridiculous to say so."

"O God!"

"Look, I'm not trying to split hairs or be sophistical and difficult. I think you must realize that this is an important question for me, and I'm looking for a way out of it that's honest—true to me, true to everybody."

"O.K., O.K., I'll try."

"You'll try to look at it from the point of view, the spiritual frame of reference of the man in the story?"

"Yes, yes, I said I'd try."

"The question is what he has to decide to do. From his point of view—this is the basic fact for him—his life is virtually over. There is, as he sees it, only one act that he can perform that will be the act of a living man in his own right and not the act of a creature invented by his brother and sister."

"Yes?"

"To kill his brother and sister."

"O!" The sound she made was almost a groan. "Why can't he just walk out and be his own man from now on?"

"He can't because, by the time he discovers the slow murder being carried out on him, he no longer has enough life left, enough independence, to do that. He has the strength to *destroy* his brother and sister, as his last, and maybe his only independent act, but he does not have the strength to *ignore* them. As long as they remain alive, they remain the guiding forces of his life, the stunting forces that render any independent action but that of killing them impossible for him. For you that condition, that aspect of the situation, namely the tremendous hold they have over him, is a mere psychological cobweb to be brushed away. That's because you don't experience it and don't feel it and have no sympathy for it and no sense of how integral it is to his entire being. For him it is no cobweb at all, but the rock on which his whole self is built."

"The self, feeding forever on its injustice! Growing fat...Arch, I know you are suffering. Maybe the thing to do is stop thinking about it for a little. You say I don't sympathize, don't feel. I do."

She took his hand that had been holding the seat of his armless chair, and he surrendered it to hers.

"You're one of the few people I've met who actually has a problem and isn't just pretending to have one for the effect. I don't know what the answer is for you. I don't see it. There's something about it that, no matter how I struggle, trying to penetrate it, escapes me. We try to hold ourselves together. . . but I know this, there comes a point where your desires and mine come together...."

"Come together?"

"It's a beautiful idea, isn't it? After all this straining and frustration...."

She moved his hand over to her lap, which he saw was covered by a large silk kerchief with a writhing paisley design.

"Aren't you hot?...under that?" he asked.

"Yes," she said, "I am." And she drew his hand under the kerchief, and he realized that she was naked under it. His fingers found themselves among coarse silky hairs. He looked down and saw her jeans on the floor—or rather, a leg of them, coming out from the chair under one of her bare feet.

"This," she said, "is what you think your brother has and what you lack. But as you can see—feel—it's easy enough to come by."

If she only hadn't mentioned my brother! thought Archibald. He thought he knew what he was going to do; but he moved his fingers about—one finger in particular—just the same: much in the manner, as Kaskin would have said, of Odysseus, passing the Island of the Sirens, who left his ears unplugged to the Sirens' song because he knew he was strapped to a headlong ship and the ship was deaf.

He drew his hand slowly, reluctantly away. "To do this—this kind of thing—after all these years would be to become a different person."

"That's lame. I need a better reason than that." Her voice was huskily saturated with the pain of desire.

"I learned fear in the army."

"Fear of what?"

"I don't know."

"You don't know. I do. I know you. You masturbate."

Her voice was getting loud, and she was beginning to thrash about under the kerchief, which Archibald was terribly afraid might slip off.

"I copulate with a ghost," he said, "the ghost of..."

"You copulate with yourself," she screamed. "You can't do it with any one or any thing but yourself! Get away from here, you self-bugger!"

Archibald stumbled to his feet, hitching his pants up tightly, as his plate of half-eaten potato salad slid to the floor. He kneeled down to scrape it together off the rug.

"Leave it!" she said, standing over him and buckling the belt on her jeans. Good God, she's quick with those things, he thought. "I'd rather clean up your mess than have you here a moment longer. Just move it. O. K.?"

Archibald got to his feet. In the room's dim light, a mere step or two carried him out of her world.

NINETEEN

He stood quietly, surveying the room about him—the various conversations, the business, the pleasure, the desire for business, the desire for pleasure. Maybe it was time to go home, he thought. But he knew that thought was false even while he was thinking it. He knew even while he was surveying the faces that there was only one face that interested him out of all the faces there—Patrick's, Timothy's, everyone's—and its faintly freckled cheekbones and quiet gray eyes were turned toward him, even now.

He took the few steps separating them, and once again stood before the ottoman on which she was sitting.

"Cynthia?"

She smiled. "You've only heard my name once. You have a good memory."

He sat down beside her in his old place. "I usually forget people's names right away, the ones I don't like. You...You don't mind my being a chauvinist?"

"Of course I mind, but every man is a chauvinist."

"And every woman?"

"The term doesn't apply to women."

"Why not?"

"Because the term was invented by women and they only apply it to men. It's like the terms invented by men that only apply to women, like 'virgin' and 'whore.' 'Chauvinist' refers to a man who wishes to perpetuate the oppression of women. How can that refer to a woman?"

"But then I'm not a chauvinist because I don't wish that, and so all men aren't chauvinists."

"You should say that you aren't aware of wishing that. No one can know exactly what he wishes in his subconscious mind. So you are in no position to deny that you are a chauvinist."

"And by the same reasoning you are in no position to assert that I am. If I don't know what wishes lurk in me, you don't either."

"I deduce your wishes from your actions."

"Can't I make the same deductions?"

"You are unwilling to. That's one of the wishes that establishes you as a chauvinist."

"You mean my very refusal to admit that I'm a chauvinist establishes the fact that I am one."

"If nothing else."

"But that...that makes me feel helpless."

"I can't help that."

"I mean helplessly and unfairly tangled in sophistries. I'm condemned either way. In the Middle Ages, they threw a woman suspected of witchcraft into a river or lake. If she drowned, she was innocent, and if she could swim, she was a witch and they killed her. Do you see any similarity?"

"None whatever. No one is drowning you or burning you at the stake, and the casualness with which you use that old horror to illustrate a harmless definition, asking me to accept them as equivalent, only makes me surer that our term is valuable."

Her voice was always quiet, measured and with a hint of melody, and he admired the simplicity and exactitude with which she expressed her views. Those qualities were part of her, and yet he had the feeling that he was not talking with her at all, but only with a set of ideas she had acquired, something mechanical and laid upon her that had, really, nothing to do with her. Her real self was in her directness, her quiet, uncompromising, almost brutal simplicity, and at the same time the kindness, the melody, the sadness that one sensed about her. Above all, the sadness. He found himself secretly hoping that their talk might hit upon something that would move them to weep together.

"That was a strange conversation I had with Patrick just now," he said.

"I saw."

"Saw?"

"Everything." She smiled almost wistfully.

"She's incredibly quick with those jeans of hers."

"Yes, practice makes perfect. She's a lovely person."

"Then she... often?"

"Most are more enticed than you seem to have been."

"But...then what?"

"There's a bedroom through there beyond the buffet."

"And she puts her jeans back on, only to..."

"Let's not go into all the silly details, unless...are you sorry you didn't take her up?"

"You mean, lay her down?"

"I don't like puns. You wanted to. Why didn't you?"

"It's difficult to explain, maybe impossible. I haven't for a long time."

"How long?"

"Twenty-four years."

"And before that?"

"The army. Some sordid things in the army. But that doesn't have much to do with it. One gets over things like that very easily, I find. But somehow I had acquired the feeling before that—and it was deepened by those things in the army—that sex ought to be only with things—people—my first sex when I was fourteen was with a mathematical problem—only with things and people that one really likes, adores, worships. That way, one isn't being pulled apart, performing an act of love and feeling distaste, revulsion even. That way, one keeps oneself in one piece.... And when I got out of the army, I realized that the only person or thing in those two years I'd felt any deep affection for was a friend who was killed, and I hadn't had any sex with him. I felt there would be nothing more—that I would never again have such feelings for anyone. So I took a vow of abstinence."

"That's very unusual in these times."

"I wonder. First of all I wonder whether I've told you the truth. If I can be a male chauvinist without realizing it, then I guess I can have sexual motivations I'm unaware of. Maybe I'm in love with my sister. Excuse me, I realize I mustn't joke about matters like that with you."

"You're free to do as you please. What else do you wonder about?"

"Whether the urge to celibacy is so unusual. It's not supposed to be. It's out of fashion. And being out of fashion can practically make a thing go out of existence—but not entirely, if it's something deep enough in people. When you think about things like that—deep-rooted things—you usually think of the so-called 'basic drives.' And these are usually listed as hunger, sex, shelter, and so on—material appetites, because the anthropologists who make up the lists have been told that they are scientists and taught to hate intangibles like dreams, hallucinations, religion. But these strange urges for intangibles—like the urge to celibacy—keep recurring, even today in this society of ours which pretends to be aware only of material gratifications. It's like that new kind of illness, so

THE INVESTIGATOR

called, that everyone is talking and writing about, where teenage girls get the urge to starve themselves."
"Anorexia Nervosa. It's a terrible illness."
"Terrible. But is it really an illness? What I mean is, is it correct to define it as something totally morbid and pathological, to be stamped out at all cost?"
"But it's a wasting, sometimes a killing disease."
"Or is it an uncontrolled outbreak of an urge that every civilization but ours has recognized and found a place for: the urge to asceticism?"
"If you had seen that disease in operation, you wouldn't want to find a place for it anywhere."
"I'm not asking anybody to bless it. I'm only asking what the best way might be to cure it—to transform it into something harmless, or maybe even beneficial. But excuse me. We got diverted. We were talking about unusual urges in these times. Do you...do you have any unusual urges?"
"No, all my urges are quite ordinary."
"But it doesn't seem at all ordinary, the way you admit—the way you say that—so calmly and unselfconsciously, with that faint smile. You seem so confident, as though you didn't have to be ashamed, or afraid, of anything."
She smiled a little more strongly than she had before, "Well, if you go on in that vein, I'll lose my unself-consciousness at least. As I said, I've all the usual urges, and that includes having an ego, being amenable to flattery...."
"And...?"
"You can fill in any of the additional details as well as I."
"Can we—would you like to go somewhere else, out of here?" He came out of his slouch against the wall on the ottoman beside her and sat up straight,

watching her expectantly and feeling more eager than he had about anything in a long time.

"Yes, we could," she said. "Why do you want to leave here? Does Patrick make you uncomfortable? She's been watching you."

"Has she? No, she doesn't bother me."

"That's callous, isn't it?"

"Is it? I've felt what she's feeling and got over it."

"You've never felt it, from what you've told me, for a person who was right there and could have made you better."

"Then it will be easier for her if I'm not here. That's callous again. I'm sorry. But what can I do? I don't think it would help if I went over and offered my apologies. But you've diverted me. She has nothing to do with why I want to leave here with you. I want to leave here with you because I want to be alone with you—and because I want to find out whether you also want to be alone with me. I don't know much of anything about you and don't seem to have the wits to find out, but in another sense I know a lot about you, maybe more than anyone has ever known, and this has made me want very much to know one final thing, whether you like me, which I haven't had the courage to ask. But if you leave with me, I'll know."

She smiled. "Yes, I like you. And I'll leave with you." They stood up together, an odd pair: he like a great bear in his baggy workpants and sweaty shirt with frayed collar and cuffs; and she a rather slight figure in an old blouse, blue denim skirt, bare legs, and sneakers.

But as they approached the door, Archibald saw George Kaskin, Jim Balam and a third person coming toward them.

"Hi Cynthia!" said Kaskin. "Are you leaving, Arch?

Before you go, I'd just like you to meet Steven Swift here. Steven is a native American, a poet, and a very interesting fellow generally."

"I'm so glad to meet you, Archibald Bromley. I've heard so much about you."

"And I, you," said Archibald lamely, beside himself with irritation. Steven was a handsome young man of slight build, very dark skin, dark eyes, American Indian nose and hairdo. The large figure of Jim Balam leaned with one hand against the door into the corridor, which opened inward into the room and was closed. There would be no getting through it without moving Balam, he thought, somewhat irrationally—and Balam would probably not move until he, Archibald, had joined Steven Swift's tribe, donned the sacred feathers, smoked the peace pipe, ceremonially painted his body, and slept with one of the chief's wives. Archibald looked up at Balam's hand plastered high on the wall, like a soft lethal octopus. Yes, he thought, that hand really is enormous.

"And Cynthia, Cynthia Madel! How nice to see you again."

"O it's wonderful to see you, Steven. I'm so glad you could come, with your busy schedule."

Archibald felt a pang. He had never heard her speak with such animation and total friendliness. It never occurred to him that was her usual tone and that the laconic, almost curt tone she used with him had been something special with her, signifying informality and openness. He felt jealous that Steven knew her whole name and he didn't and anguished when they both leaned forward and embraced each other with a hearty, friendly kiss.

I really know nothing about her, he thought, feeling hopeless. Everyone here knows her better than I do.

They talked. They talked endlessly about poems, pow-wows, potlatches—Archibald couldn't remember what. He never knew. He forgot every sentence, including his own, which were the most forgettable of all, as soon as uttered. Marvelous how the mind works, he mused. The things it can pick out and unerringly consign to eternal oblivion. The only thing he remembered, and he could not think of anything in recent years that had caused him more pain, was Cynthia's easy simple enjoyment of every word that was said.

But at last the octopus unstuck its suckers from the door, the door opened, and Cynthia and Archibald were released into the night.

TWENTY

They stood on the sidewalk. "Where shall we go?" he asked, perhaps with a touch of bitterness in his voice, not sure now that he wanted to go anywhere with this simple-minded creature who had such an interest in American Indians and their ancient wrongs, their age-old sufferings, the massacres of their tribes, the white man's injustice and hypocrisy—as though one people before this in the whole history of the earth had never conquered and exterminated another. They didn't exterminate Steven Swift, did they? Why didn't they?

She smiled. "I guess I didn't tell you. I have a place two blocks from here."

A wave of warmth swept through him, totally changing his mood. What power she has, he thought, by altering my surroundings, to alter me! That, he recognized, was a very familiar kind of thought for him to have;

and for a brief moment he understood why, as a child, he had felt that the world was a mere appearance put there to control him: it was because he loved the world and resented the power it had over him by virtue of his loving it. It was his mother he loved. She had made the world, and she was dead. And now the world was dead. Almost.

They walked slowly in the warm night, her feet making no sound on the pavement.

"No, I don't read much," she said, answering his question. "I don't seem to have the time, or don't take the time."

"Your work?"

"Menial. I'm not very interesting."

As with her remark earlier, that she had only ordinary urges, he was awed by the way she said this. There was none of the false irony that is almost inevitable in such statements. He was almost frightened by the detachment, the total lack of concern for her own identity.... How did she achieve it? What extraordinary experience had she gone through to make it possible? She obviously wasn't very interested in helping him find out.

"My sister gave me a good mystery to read the other day," he said. "Usually I don't much like mysteries. The people in them are so unreal that the elaborate questions about them don't seem worth answering. But in this case the people seemed very real. A man, a professor in a college, had been living for years in the same way with his wife and daughter. There had been no sex for a long time, and the wife was having an affair. The story starts when she leaves him for her lover, and he is left—plunged into himself. He is suspected of a crime, and an old crime he thinks he may have committed threatens him even more. When he is going around the town, checking on his past, he meets a waitress in a little restaurant, and she is quite uncanny—has a simplicity, a forthrightness that cuts away the nonsense, the crippling obsessions that encrust his life. A person of his own kind could never have done that."

She was putting her key in her lock and turned to him. "You mustn't expect too much of me," she said.

It was yet another two-family house—or rather, three-family, counting her as one in her small apartment in the basement. There was a tidy sitting room in which a frameless bed with a blue and red bedspread and cushions against a wall served as a divan. A table, straight-backed chairs... it was all very bare, almost austere. One door led to a small kitchen, another probably to a bedroom.

"If I make some tea, would you like some, or would you like something else?"

"Tea would be fine."

Noting with a touch of satisfaction that he didn't miss the bourbon, he let his eyes wander about the room. The only books he could see were between bookends on a table to his right' a few paperbacks and, in hardcover, The New York Social Register and "Today on Wall Street." What possessed her to acquire books like that? On the wall to the left a gray and gold tapestry....

"You didn't like Steven Swift, did you?" she said from the kitchen.

"Did that show?" he said, looking in at the kitchen door. He admired the sureness and delicacy with which she worked—particularly as he sensed that her handling of the spoons, cups, and kettle was not deeply accustomed: she would have had the same grace, doing anything with those thin wrists and pale hands. He wanted to take them and kiss them. He felt awkward. She might be more than twenty years younger than he. It was as though his years in the house on Clairmont Street were the gulf between them.

"It wasn't that I disliked him, personally or any other way," he said. "It was just that I sensed him as an obstacle, keeping me from standing here, watching you make tea."

"It was your impatience that showed, then. But he may have taken it for something else."

"Did I really make such a poor job of hiding my feelings?"

"I don't know. He may not have noticed."

"Does it matter what he noticed? I'm sorry. Callous again."

"He's very sensitive."

"Is he a male chauvinist? Excuse me again. A facetious remark. But aren't we all sensitive—just as we are all chauvinists—all the males, at least?"

"No, we are not all sensitive."

"You mean, I'm not."

"I didn't say that."

"How do I get out of this trap you have sprung on me?"

"You shouldn't get out. You should savor being there and think about how you got there."

"How?"

"By never being able to forget yourself."

"With you I can." He moved toward her.

"I doubt it. And even if you can, that's not enough."

"I love you, Cynthia."

The water had boiled. She poured it into the teapot and took the tray out into the other room. When she had set it on the long, low table in front of the divan and sat down herself, she looked up at him and said, "That's not enough either. If your love accepts being unkind to a person who has done you no harm, then it's not enough."

"Your standards are high." He sat down beside her and took a cup.

"So are yours."

"But I'm on the verge of crimes."

"We all are."

"Are we? What crimes are you about to commit?" He thought he saw a twinkle of mirth in her eyes as she said, "You're going to get tired of hearing this answer. Only the ordinary ones. They aren't interesting."

"You're playing with me, refusing to tell me anything about yourself. You're playing some kind of game that I don't understand."

"It's no game. Believe me."

Her eyes, her whole face, on him when she said this were so steady, so totally sober, that she seemed to be carved in stone.

"Because you seem," he said, "as though you might be a way out for me, might help me make things alright again.... You have a simplicity.... You don't seem to have to worry about preserving yourself, your honor. You always just seem to accept and endure. And that makes you seem indestructible."

"You see a lot in me."

"In your face. It has a smile on it that never seems to disappear completely—like those Egyptian statues in the Museum—and the steady eyes. That's it. You look sometimes as though you had been carved in Ancient Egypt."

"That's the nicest thing that's been said to me in a long time," she said with a touch of mirth. "I'll remember that."

"I know I'm clumsy. You asked me what I saw in

you. That's what I saw. That's what you mean to me. Don't play with me."

"Don't you with me. You arrange everything, every detail in your world, to suit yourself. That's how you delude yourself."

"You're warning me, I suppose. I'm grasping, seeing things. I can't help it. Am I wrong about you, then—the kind of person you are?"

She was silent.

"Can't you tell me?" he asked.

"I'm afraid to."

"Why?"

"You've grown dependent. That's especially frightening to me."

She looked down at him from her erect position near the edge of the bed, where he sat against the wall with his legs drawn up close to his chin.

"You always get into the fetal position."

"That's rubbish!" he cried, letting go of his knees and springing forward, so that he was sitting upright beside her. "I'm getting tired of this. I am being played with. It is some kind of game with you. I don't know how or why, but it is."

"I love you. Is that a game?"

TWENTY-ONE

He was stunned.

"I'm new to love," he said. "I've read that love is the creation of images. And being new to it, though I'm so old, maybe I've been making up the images too thickly, too heavily. Am I dreaming this?"

He took her hand. "I wanted to touch this when you were in the kitchen. And wanted to kiss it." He

kissed it. "It's real. It's a little cold, but it's real....
Will you marry me? Will you come and live with
me? There are some things I'll have to explain...."
  "I've heard about your living arrangements."
  "You mean my brother and sister, the big house,
the servant's room?"
  "Yes."
  "But how? From Kaskin? He told you?"
  "He told several of us."
  "Why?"
  "He wasn't making fun. It's the kind of person he
is."
  He felt a new kind of terror—or was it an old kind?—
and his eyes, rolling about, lighted on different objects in the room: the social register, the tapestry, a silver dish on a little table under it that he hadn't noticed before, that seemed to have been put there since he last looked. At last his eyes returned to her and held her gloomily. Did she look frightened? He asked, separating his words slowly and deliberately:
  "Is George Kaskin the Devil?"
  Her face drew together, then relaxed. Then he heard her laugh out loud for the first time. It was a lovely, clear sound that almost made him forget the agony that had driven him to ask the question.
  "You *are* a little insane!" she said finally, "I'll tell him you asked."
  "I mean...that's not as crazy as it sounds. I had reasons for saying it that weren't completely irrational."
  "Yes, I'm sure you did. I can almost see it. The mad little beard, the wild hair and popping eyes. And the red face. I think George may drink a little too much."
  "No, I mean much more than that. I mean things that happened. At the poetry reading, that poetess..."

"Don't say 'poetess' any more. Just say poet."
"Sybil...I forget her last name."
"Maypole."
"She read this poem that was all about my situation, my problem. It couldn't have been a coincidence. There were too many details, all going together. But when I asked him about it, he swore he had nothing to do with it, swore on his honor as a human being, or some such thing, since he didn't believe in God and so couldn't swear to God."
"The Devil believes in God."
"And so I say, Maybe you're not a human being. Maybe you're the Devil. And he says, Yes, maybe he is."
"Wait a moment. It's not like George to tell outright untruths. You say he said he had *nothing* to do with it?"
"Well... not exactly. I accused him of having written the poem himself (Poem. Why am I calling it a poem? It was garbage.) and having Sybil read it."
"First of all, you've got to know that no one ever *has* Sybil Maypole do anything. But the important thing is about George. You accused him of that, and he denied it, and that was all?"
"I think so."
"Then he was telling the truth."
"Who wrote it, then?"
"Sybil. If it was garbage, as you say, she must have written it."
"O, we can be mean, after all, can't we?"
"Yes, I'm sorry, Sybil's a sweet person, and I love her dearly. And she understands clearly enough that she is not to read me any more of her poems."
"But I still don't understand."
"George told a group of us about you one evening—

not in an unkind way at all. You know that confidential, case-study manager he has, as though he were the consulting psychologist at a spy trial. And something else you have to know about him too. He used to be an actor for a little while, studied it anyway, and he loves to put on little shows, weave harmless plots. When he told us about you, he didn't think we would ever see you, so you have to excuse him for being indiscreet. Then someone suggested (It *was* Sybil, I think. She's always eager to crowd people into her readings.) that we invite you there—and then to Balam's later. Still no one thought you'd come. And when you did, George was true to his nature and couldn't resist being playful. That explains his truthful but unhelpful answer to you. Sybil must have written the poem on her own, probably without even knowing that you were coming. That makes perfect sense. The poor dear writes poems about everything. If she has a corn on her big toe, she writes a poem about it.... But what I don't understand either is why she read that poem about you, knowing that you were there. Because I meant it when I said that about her. She really is a very nice person. She did know that you actually were there, I suppose?"

He clapped the palm of his hand against his forehead and gave that quick little explosive laugh which registers sudden illumination. "I'll say she knew. I interrupted her introduction with a snide remark. And she knew it was me because I was sitting next to Kaskin—to George."

"Interrupted her with a snide remark and in front of all her followers? O, that was unforgivable."

"And so, direly provoked...."

"She paid you back."

"Brilliantly."

"Brilliantly. At last Sybil has risen to greatness."
There were tears in his eyes. He could feel them.
He leaned forward and took her in his arms and kissed her chastely on the mouth, as one kisses a sister.
"Thank you," he said.
She pushed him lightly away and looked at him seriously and carefully.
"So will you marry me?" he repeated. "Will you come and live with me in my servant's room? But we can change that. Even move out of there."
"Even?"
"Definitely. We'll definitely move out of there, if you like. There's money. And I want to get a job."
"I can't marry you."
"Can't...."
"I have to tell you...do you know who I am?"
"You're..." His voice faltered. "You're Cynthia Madel—two names, the first learned from quick-on-the-draw Patrick, the fastest cunt on the West Side, and the last from Tonto, an obnoxious Indian. High-O, Silver! A melodious but silly name, which I hope will shortly be improved by being changed, flying in the face of all your feminist views, to Cynthia Bromley. Why is that tear rolling down your cheek?"
"Give me something more definite, something more descriptive of the person you have been talking with all evening. A sociological sketch will do." The strain was audible in her voice.
He looked around the apartment. "A person of moderate means. A menial job, she says. Pathologically secretive about herself. Of humble origins probably. Poor study habits. Penetrating intelligence. Uncanny capacity to transform the lives of others—me, for instance, whom she has turned, not to stone, but to a

wide river flowing—turned me to a poet, which I have not ever been before and shall never be again. Stop crying before I start to."

"The name, Madel, means nothing to you?"

"Only what I have said. What am I to think of? The newspapers?"

"Oscar Madel."

"The toothpaste tycoon?"

"I'm Cynthia Madel, the toothpaste heiress, and I'm worth seventeen million dollars."

"Can't you throw them away? Give them away?"

"No, I can't. I've tried. George says they are like the burning shirt someone puts on in a Greek play: the more you try to tear it off, the deeper it burns into your flesh. I can't destroy my fortune without destroying myself."

"And so like me, clinging to my injuries, you cling to your money."

"That's why I understand you so well."

"And those people at the party? Do they know?"

"They're lovely people. They forget who I am, or pretend to."

"But why didn't you tell me before—in the beginning?"

"If I had told you in the beginning, would the few hours we've known each other have been like this?"

"No, I guess not."

"And are you sorry the hours have been as they were?"

"No."

"Then you see why we can't go on, now that you know."

"Because everything will be different now? No, I don't see! There have been stranger unions."

"And more monstrous ones. The corruption has already set in. Already I have begun to suspect your motives for not seeing. And shortly you would begin to suspect them too."

"That's vile. I loved you."

"Already it's in the past tense. And besides, I could never compete with your true love."

"My true love?"

"Clara."

"You're trying to disgust me. You just think I'm too old and peculiar. An oddity. An amusement... I'm sorry.... Don't cry."

He put his head in his hands, elbows on his knees, fingers in his hair and stared at the floor, and they were silent a long time. Then he looked up and said,

"You'll be moving out of here and into a larger place soon?"

"Yes."

"Where?"

"Near Kaskin's."

"A big house in that posh-academic district?"

"Yes."

"You've decided to accept the life that has been laid out for you?"

"Yes."

"And I should do the same in mine," he said, more to himself than to her, and hung his head again. Then, looking up, he said, "We sit here in our prisons.... Faust says to the Devil in the old play, 'What are you doing out of Hell?' And the Devil answers, 'Wherever I am is Hell, and I'm never out of it.' You got yourself this little working girl's flat and try to be ordinary and uninteresting, but you can't ever get out. And I saw you and thought that you might help me escape from myself. But it's too late. I'll never get out of myself. So I'd better go back and establish my brother's and sister's guilt."

"You already have, and you have already sentenced them."

"Yes, the final act. Can I make love to you before I leave?"

"I don't think you really want to break your vows for me."

"And you?"

"Sometimes."

"It hurts me to think of it."

They had been looking away in their separate directions. But now she looked at him, and he saw that her face was losing its composure.

"We might have grown old together," she said, "decayed together. Your teeth would have begun to fall out, then mine. We would have comforted each other. I would have been sadder about yours than mine, you sadder about mine than yours."

They sat in silence a little while longer. Then he got up, kissed her on the forehead, and went out the front door.

TWENTY-TWO

Archibald decided to walk home. He was not absolutely sure about the direction and thoroughly vague about the distance, but it didn't matter. He had plenty of time. He could stop at lunch counters and sleep on park benches and under bridges. The dawn was beginning, promising a fine day, not overly hot—though that didn't matter either. So he knew where the east was, and therefore the west also, and he was quite sure that Sweethill lay westward. He was in good physical condition. It might be good to walk. It might be good to keep walking for as long as he lived.

His fingertips assured him that the fresh-cut key was still in his pocket, the duplicate he had made the day before of the key sent to Edward and Clara for their vacation cottage on the Cape. In a sense it was the key to his prison, the latest key, and it gave him a feeling of comfort. Safe behind bars.

But as he walked the lengths of an endless succession of hot streets and shimmering avenues, he began to picture that key as a magical talisman, or as a science-fictional mysterious electronic power button, drawing him infallibly and irresistibly to his destination and his destiny. He need not stop and ask for directions: he need only heed the subliminal twitchings of the key against his thigh. The hickory stick twitched in the dowser's hand, revealing the hidden water below: thus the key, Archibald's pocket, and his destiny.

Then why couldn't he wrench it, squirming like a large beetle, from his pocket and fling it on its way, and himself turn around, retrace his steps, and reenter the world he had left? Himself? What self, when the key was gone? No, he had been through all this before with Cynthia.... He mustn't utter that name. It would drive him mad—if he was not mad already.

He lost track of time. He was hungry. But he liked the feeling: a friendly warm gnawing in his gut that seemed to be purifying him, making him lighter. In the army he had first noticed that going hungry dampened his sexual appetite, and so he had stayed thin for years, but in his forties the necessity had grown less imperious and he had put on weight. He'd better watch himself, though. He'd better get back into training. Look what had almost happened last night!

So he would fast as well as walk. He would walk

through the city as Gandhi had through India. And in some ways he cut as strange a figure as the great Mahatma when the sun rose in the sky and he lost sight of familiar landmarks and grew uncertain of the direction: for then he had to swing up in his baggy pants to some magazine seller or fruit vendor and ask, "Could you tell me the direction to Sweethill?"

"Sweet what?"

"Sweet Hill. The suburb."

"O yeah, Sweethill! The suburb! Now you're talking. Well, I think your best bet would be to backtrack here, two blocks down and one over at the light and catch the subway to Grub Street. Then at Grub Street you can hop on the Pink Line to..."

"I'm not using public transportation. I'm walking."

"Walking! To Sweethill? You crazy or something? Look, would you just move along and let me get on with selling these apples and lemons? I've had it with all these marches in support of every goddam thing— syphilitic pygmies in Outer Mongolia, untrained heartburn in Inner Bellyache. It was work that made America beautiful and not all this crying over spilt causes."

After a few replies of that sort, he took to asking more simply, "Pardon me, could you tell me which direction is west?.

"You see that big bright light hung up there in the sky? It's headed west. Just follow it. *Follow thy fair sun, unhappy shadow!"*

> But soft! What light on yonder pavement bakes?
> It is the west, and Archibald is the sun!
> Arise, fair sun, and kill the envied pair,
> Who are already sick and pale with grief.

Actually it wasn't that long a walk—no more than

ten miles, even in the erratic way he walked it. By mid morning he came to the river, spanned by familiar bridges, whose banks were studded with well-known landmarks, and he would have been home by early afternoon if he hadn't fallen asleep in a riverside park, numbed by the roar of traffic and lulled by the lap of the river on nearby stones. He lay on a patch of grass, feeling weak and ethereal from lack of food. It was strange to shut his eyes one moment and then, opening them the next, to discover that the sun had leapt across the sky, making different shadows around the nearby trees, buildings, bridge. And there was one completely different shadow standing directly over him. A tall black man.

"Yes?"

"Power!"

"Black Power?"

"Edgar Allan Poe Power!"

Archibald rolled over toward the man and, putting one elbow on the ground, propped his head with his forearm. A little later he swung his legs in front of him and sat up. The man standing over him was in the prime of early manhood: a beautifully shaped head under its kinky hair, a broad shiny forehead, high cheekbones, strong jaw; and he had broad shoulders, narrow hips. But he was not a pleasant sight. Of his lower teeth, only the two canines remained, poking awkwardly from the pale wet pinkness of his gums, and there were no upper teeth at all. He swayed back and forth as he spoke, and sometimes gave little lunges, as of a dancing prize fighter, in one direction or another. A pair of green pants remarkably like Archibald's clung uncertainly to his hips, but the black man's were streaked with innumerable stains. He stank of urine and sweat, and perhaps a touch of stale vomit.

Archibald was fascinated. There was something deeply satisfying in this, something to which he felt personally akin. He too had begun well.

"Poe Power. I have Poe Power. Edgar Allan Poe Power. You know what I mean?"

"The name is familiar. He wasn't a civil rights activist, was he?"

The man swayed and squinted at him through deeply bloodshot eyes. Archibald felt ashamed of himself.

"Civil wipe my...." said the man. "On a midnight dark and weary.... Sir, could you let me have a half dollar as a contribution...." He belched. "...toward a small container of Musca...?"

"I'm broke. Haven't got a cent in my pockets."

The man closed his eyes in disgust and irony. "Thou hast denied me twice."

"Nor hath the cock crowed," said Archibald with a smile, and thought: How can he eat with just those two teeth like that—the canines, the deep-rooted ones that last the longest when the gums loosen and bleed, the bone rots, and the teeth begin to wobble in their sockets. He'd be able to eat better on just his gums.

He held out a hand, stooping, to Archibald, who crouched, ready to scramble for safety if the man should fall on him.

"Thrice!" said the black man.

Archibald cursed his father, whom he was imitating now and who never gave money to beggars because he never felt—or pretended never to feel—the need to propitiate the less fortunate who had not gone to Harvard nor been trained as brain surgeons. Trained, the voice of Kaskin reminded him, largely by Government subsidy: that is, by the very pennies extracted as liquor tax from this toothless man when he bought the sickening swill sold to him under the name of wine.... What had most deeply shocked the Indians about the white man, according to their own testimony in a book Kaskin had lent him, was that the white man seemed to feel no need to propitiate the foes he had destroyed. 'You have not even asked our ghosts for forgiveness,' they said, 'and when you think you are alone in the years to come, in your cities or in your forests, you will not be alone, but our angry ghosts will be swarming about you.'

He looked up and saw, shiny in the afternoon sunlight, dancing behind, to the side, and in front of the black man, smaller than life, the lithe spidery figure of Steven Swift. This little newcomer to the scene had a band around his forehead and a single feather protruding from his hair. His limbs and body, the color of ash but with a high polish, were naked except for a breechcloth like that worn by Mahatma Gandhi or a newborn baby, and in his hand, ready to shoot an arrow, was a little white curved bow, of the kind that Cupid carries on cheap valentines. As the black man spoke, this little Steven Swift (Archibald recognized him immediately as an hallucination) moved his lips too, in silent kissing motions, and Archibald could read what they said, over and over again,

'You didn't propitiate my spirit, so I kept you from your love. You didn't propi...'

—while the love-hate arrows, twinging like Sybil Maypole's twingies from the little white bow, stung his eyes and cheeks, and the black man spoke,

"I have Poe Power, Edgar Allan Poe Power. On a midnight dark and weary...the power of Poe is in me, and I AM the Lord...."

Archibald staggered to his feet and fought back.

"On a midnight dark with wee-wee..."

"I AM THE LORD!" the black man screamed, "and

thou shalt bow down and worship at my feet. MY FEET!"

He lurched forward. Archibald sprang back, took his wallet from his pocket, pulled out some bills, and flung them at the black man's feet. The black man lunged for them, and Archibald heard from behind, as he walked, almost ran, on his way,

"Thank you, Marstah! Thank you, Lord Jesus, Marstah, thank you!"

TWENTY-THREE

The sun was beginning to slope deeply from the zenith and the afternoon had weakened when Archibald found his car—in the shade luckily—got into it, slumped in the seat and felt fatigue, like a great river, washing over him. He closed his eyes, yielding to it, and slowly it receded. Perhaps because he was back now in the world of mechanical contrivances, he brought his wristwatch in front of his eyes to check the time before he remembered that the watch had run down last night and he had not bothered to wind and set it. It would be around four, he judged, and he would be home long before five-thirty, that is, long before Edward and Clara. Not even considering whether or not he would stop at Kaskin's house a few yards down the street, he drove off.

To his surprise, Edward's little green Mercury and Clara's Cadillac were both in the driveway. On Thursday? he wondered, pulling up behind Edward. He wasn't fully out from behind the wheel when they both appeared at the front door, and as he was rounding the rear bumper, Clara, rushing out to meet him, flung her arms around his neck and said tearfully, "Archie!"

He was surprised. It must have been ten years and more since she had last touched him in affection. She had a loveliness about her still, he thought fleetingly, and "Clara, your true love," he remembered Cynthia saying in that other world. But he was home now.
"How come you're home so early? Isn't this a workday?"
"A workday!" she said, her voice breaking. "It was the first day in more than twenty years that I didn't know where my little brother, Archie, was. Even when you had that pneumonia and almost died, I knew where you were—where your body was anyway. Your spirit was traveling to strange continents. Archie, you really mustn't do this again, or you must let us know. We had no idea where you were. Where were you?"
"She was really beside herself, Arch," said Edward. "No comforting her."
"But.... I'd only gone to a poetry reading."
"That's just it," said Clara. "How long can you spend at a poetry reading?"
"O I don't know..." said Edward, who, when challenged, liked to assert that poetry was important.
"We went to a party afterward."
"Was it nice?"
"It was O.K."
"I hope you didn't do anything scandalous!" They all stood silent when Clara said that, intending to sound light-hearted and bantering. The incident at the Contis was still casting its shadow. Finally Archibald replied,
"No, sweetheart, I didn't do anything scandalous."
"Archie, I'm sorry."
"Don't be sorry. I know I've become suspicious..." he paused for an instant, sensing the double meaning, "after the evening at the Contis. So it's right to suspect me of things."

"We've forgotten the evening at the Contis!" she said.

"You mustn't. You've got to be aware of the risks. When you put your arms around me and welcome me home, you may be like Cleopatra, clasping the viper to her bosom."

Clara surprised him by smiling at this, pushing playfully against his chest with the palm of her hand, and saying, "I'm not going to *listen* to nonsense like that!"

Suddenly it seemed to Archibald that his remark about the viper was like King Kong, the giant ape in the old movie, clinging to the top of the Empire State Building while toy-sized aircraft from the Army Air Corps made puny strafing runs at him and eventually brought him down. Edward came in at another angle:

"Yes, Arch, your comparison to Cleopatra does seem a little overdramatic to me."

Archibald grinned. "I guess I am full of outlandish comparisons today."

"Well, what are we standing here for?" said Clara. "Archie, you look awful. Are you going to get cleaned up for dinner? We're going to have a real dinner tonight, I've decided. Steak, french-fries, the works. So come on, let's get going."

They went in through the front door. Clara turned left toward the kitchen, saying, "There's no great hurry, though. Still some unfreezing to do," and the brothers drifted to the bar.

"Drink, Arch?"

"No thanks."

"Well, maybe it *is* a bit early," he said, and they went into the library.

"Clara's really in her jaunty mood," said Archibald, "I'm not sure I know exactly what to make of it."

"Well, you know we're going on our vacation on Saturday—just the day after tomorrow—the vacation you so graciously insisted that we take. That might explain it."

"But it doesn't."

"Yes, well, no, perhaps it doesn't.... Truth is, your sister has been about as upset last night and today as I have ever seen her. Especially today, when..."

"...when she discovered that I hadn't come back from my visit with that vile George Kaskin, who was showing me all the kingdoms of the Earth."

Edward's beautiful eyes twinkled. "Yes, your raggedy Mephistopheles. That seems to have been the trigger."

"She was afraid I might sign a pact with him."

"I wish I knew what she was afraid of. You know, she's always been a very frightened person. A strong person, but also a frightened person. Maybe the two qualities go together. You wouldn't guess it, but so often they seem to. I think a lot in Clara's case stems from her attraction—from how terrifically attractive she was as a girl. She really was beautiful. In many ways she still is—I guess the classic face, the coloring—dark eyes, light hair...you remember, don't you, how she used to refuse to pluck her eyebrows? Extraordinary effect. Meeting between her eyes. Like something wild."

How carried away you are, dear brother, thought Archibald.

"And you remember too, I guess, how every male in a ten mile radius used to chase after her, but I doubt you ever realized how deeply she hated such attentions."

"But she confessed her feelings to you, of course."

"Yes, of course. I was her older brother, and we

were devoted.... But she was violently shy with everyone—every male, even me. Afraid, I suspect, of the power she had over us—over them."

Yes, thought Archibald, afraid of the very thought of sex because the only male she wanted was Edward and sex with him was unthinkable—at least in those early days of innocence.

"When did it begin?" said Archibald in a voice so loud that Edward was startled.

"O yes. Forgive me for digressing. This resurgence lately of all her old fears and revulsions. Your little night on the town seems to have triggered it, as I said; but it may—it probably has nothing to do with you. Actually it began before that, I think."

"What exactly do you mean by 'it'?"

"Well, you see—you mustn't laugh—I can see you're not about to—she's afraid there's a strange man in the house. In the attic. It's odd, isn't it? She's always had that tendency. She's very chaotic in some ways, Arch. You ought to see her room. She keeps it locked. I don't see it very often myself. But about other things, things that feed her fears, she can be amazingly precise. Every morning when she leaves the second floor (she insists that I go downstairs first), she leaves the bathroom door ajar and takes note of the particular tile it's touching when you look at it from a particular angle. Well, last week she got home and noticed—or believed she noticed—that the door wasn't in the same position. Which reminds me—I've been meaning to ask you: you didn't happen to go up there for any reason last week—it would have been the day after our last big evening?" By "big evening" Edward meant one in which they had stayed up late, talking and drinking after dinner.

"No," said Archibald casually, "I don't think I've

been up there in months."

"Well, it's a mystery, then. The wind—God knows what. But she was most upset about it and decided there must be a man in the attic."

"Did you look?"

"She wouldn't hear of it. She said if there was someone up there, he was undoubtedly violent, and I could only get myself killed. So in that way it just sort of hung, gradually fading, or rather, gradually seeming more and more unlikely, as the days passed and he didn't attack anybody and didn't send down for hamburgers or a chamber pot.... But then when you hadn't come back this morning, he reappeared again—or rather, his presence reasserted itself."

"The little man who wasn't there—"

"The other night upon the stair."

"He wasn't there again today."

"I wish to God he'd go away! But Arch, this is a serious business."

"Yes, it is."

"She was afraid that if we went to work and you weren't here, the man in the attic could get out and replenish his food supply."

"And empty his chamber pot."

"I suppose."

"And reassert his presence by moving the bathroom door again."

"Yes. She was very upset about you being gone too, you understand. It was as if the little man was useful in expressing her feelings about you."

"And as if I were useful in expressing her feelings about the little man."

"That too, perhaps."

"In fact it may be, Ed, that the little man and I are the same person."

"If you don't mind, Arch, things seem to be confused enough already, without you trying to confuse them even more with remarks like that."

"Sorry, Ed."

"You seem a little heartless sometimes. I know you're not really. But sometimes you seem that way."

"You're right. I don't know what it is. It's just that sometimes I get carried away by a train of thought, dominated by it, so that I myself hardly seem to exist. So then I follow it, the hunch, the inkling, the suspicion, maybe reckless sometimes about the consequences."

"It's your genius. You know, as I've said many times, I suppose, you've always seemed to us to have a touch of genius... Your pranks, your inventions...."

"Yes, you always encouraged me in them, didn't you? You and Clara?"

"O yes, we... I admired them tremendously. Things I'd just never have thought of. And you so much younger."

"And especially the ones at Queensbury, the ones I told you about before you left for the Pacific during the War. The one I was planning with the electricity. You said I really ought to go ahead with it."

"Did I? I forget. It really was bad advice if I did, wasn't it?"

"Yes, it really was."

"Arch, you don't hold me responsible in any way for your misfortunes at Queensbury, do you?"

Archibald looked carefully into the endless kindness and tenderness aglitter in Edward's big brown eyes and he found it impossible to keep his ill-will.

"No, Ed, of course not." And besides, he didn't want Edward too much on his guard.

"So then there's Clara to think about."

"You haven't gone into the attic?"

"She made me promise, Arch, made me solemnly promise that I wouldn't."

"But she hasn't made me promise, has she?"

"Hasn't thought of it yet, I suppose."

"Well, then. I'll see you later, old buddy." And as if he wanted nothing more than a little exercise after too sedentary a day, Archibald sprang from his armchair and trotted off.

TWENTY-FOUR

He paused in the hall in momentary indecision. There was no doubt in his mind that he would actually climb up to the attic on the absurd errand of making sure that Clara's strange man was not hiding there. He would make that effort—and he *was* feeling weary after his long walk and his fast—because it was easier to tell the truth than to lie. He was sure there was no one there, so there was no need to check, but Clara would not believe there was no one there unless she believed that he had been there, and he could assure her that he had gone to the attic much more convincingly if he had actually done so. He was no novelist, after all.

No, it was not that. It was simply that he did not want to lie to his sister. He didn't mind planning her death by fire, but telling her a lie was too much.

No, it was not that either. He couldn't care less about lying to his sister, and if his adventures of the last few days had convinced him of anything, it was that he had the talent to do it. No, there was something else. He had already had one hallucination today. He had no reason to believe that the black man in the park did not belong to that world of ordinary, rationally consistent phenomena that come under the heading of "reality" nowadays; but the little half-sized replica of Steven Swift dancing around the black man was clearly another matter—clearly was a specimen of a reality of a different sort. And if him, why not also Clara's stranger? How could he coldly and confidently dismiss her hysterical belief when he himself had been the host of such a hot little spook? Maybe he had *better* check that there was no one there.

But his indecision was about which way to get to the attic: by the front or the back stairs? The back stairs were his, so to speak, and the familiar, the emotionally smoother way, but the path to them led through the kitchen, where Clara would undoubtedly be, getting that special dinner she had promised, and he didn't want to meet Clara. She might ask him where he was going. He could simply say, "to my room." But she might tell him about the stranger in the attic and make him promise not to go there. And that would be very awkward: promising her, then breaking the promise, then telling her that he had—for her own good, of course.

But if he went by the front stairs and she did happen to be in her room and with her door open, then he would have no reason to be there whatsoever, and the awkwardness would be extreme.

Then why was he taking the front stairs? He had already slowly, wearily mounted the first steps. Maybe only because—as Sir Edmund Hillary said of Mount Everest—the front staircase was there. So much that was unexpected and out of place had already happened these past few days, why not this too?

He reached the second floor hall and proceeded across it to get to the next flight. When he came to Clara's door, suddenly it opened, and she appeared with her eyes wide and her lips parted. She was dressed only in a thin cotton shift and, Archibald imagined, brassiere and panties underneath.

"Ed...O...What are...Hello, Archie. I heard you coming up the stairs. It sounded like Ed—his walk. You were..."

"Yes, I was walking slowly. I'm tired. I've done a lot of walking today. There was something I wanted to get from my old room on the third floor, and I happened to be in the front hall, and so I thought..."

"You don't have to explain, dear. This house is yours as much as ours. You have every right to be here."

But Archibald knew that something terrible had happened. He had violated something, an immemorial custom, a privacy. In yet another place the subtle fabric of their life together had been torn. He did not belong here and should not have been let out, released from his lower depth, his jungle. It wasn't proper for him to observe her like this any more than it was fitting for King Kong, the giant gorilla, to hold that girl, endlessly screaming in the palm of his hand. Why didn't Clara scream? Did he want her to? Why did he?

It was for Edward that her eyes were bright, her lips parted, her body almost naked. She had something to say to him, something tender and passionate, that she had almost choked on when she saw this sweaty, stubbled creature, this consorter with drunken, toothless Negroes. He strode past her and put his foot on the first step of the next flight.

"Archie!"

He paused, turned, and she was standing beside him.

"Actually I'm glad that we've met here like this."

"Actually?"

"Well, I was a little surprised at first. You know, I don't think you've been up this way in the last twenty years or so."

"It was probably better that way, don't you think?"

"I don't know why."

"Customs, privacies develop, and people come to rely on them."

"Too much sometimes...Archie, I'm worried..."

He braced himself to hear about the man in the attic.

"There's a strange...you've become like a stranger to us, Archie. O I don't mean your little exploits and adventures. There have always been those. We can live with those. The Contis—even hanging out with that Kaskin person. We can accept that. That's you."

"What can't you accept?"

"There's nothing we can't accept. It's just that—O I don't know—there's such a strangeness that's gotten into you."

"You've said that."

"There! That's what I mean! When you say things like that. You didn't use to say things like that—so cold, so distant. I used to know what you were thinking."

She stood close to him, and he was aware of her heavy breathing under the slip. He wanted to take her, to master her, to obliterate every strangeness, every distance there ever was or would be between them. Why had he never admitted to himself that he felt this way? Something Cynthia had called out of his depths....

"I'm not thinking anything..." he said.

And why hadn't she mentioned the man in the attic? Because he was the man in the attic, who came into existence for her only when he, the actual Archibald, was absent. He felt sick. Things were coming apart.

"I was only thinking of something in my old room, a scale model of a World War One airplane I made a

THE INVESTIGATOR

long time ago—before I was even really interested in mathematics—a Fokker D-VII. I wanted to get it and put it on the bookcase in my room, instead of the rubberbandball."

"I hate that rubberbandball!"

"When you were a little girl, you used to hate the Fokker D-VII."

"Did I? Yes, I suppose I would have. I must have been intolerant. We haven't given you a very fair shake, have we, Archie?"

"We? You and Edward?"

"Yes, we haven't appreciated, didn't see, didn't understand....There's so much to say, and I don't seem able to say any of it. You're such a stranger. I know I've said that! But I can't seem to put it any better than that, express what I'm afraid of....I seem to have forgotten something...can't remember what it is."

What you have forgotten, he thought, is that not many days ago you knew, or you almost knew, that I actually suspected you and Edward. But you were drunk, and you've forgotten. And there you are, coming to pieces, trying to remember. Archibald felt overwhelmed by the horror of Clara beginning to disintegrate before his eyes.

"You'll feel better, sweetheart, when you and Ed have been away at the Cape for a few days—a lot better."

"I don't *want* to go to the Cape! *That's* what I'm afraid of! I don't want to leave you, Archie. We never go anywhere, so why are we starting now? We already have a house that's too big for us, with rooms everywhere that we never go into. Can't we be content with what we have? What'll you eat all by yourself?"

"I already eat by myself most of the time and do

most of my own cooking."

"I've been a poor sister to you...."

"No you haven't! I've preferred it that way. You know that, dear. I'll have the time of my life here alone. You and Ed go with a light heart. You need it. You need some time by yourselves. Relief from the mad stranger lurking in all the strange rooms! Look, Clara, dear. I know I'm odd—very odd: and I know you are worried about my stability. But you needn't. You mustn't. When have I ever harmed anyone?"

"There's always a first time. O, I'm sorry, Archie!"

"That's alright, dear. I understand." He placed his hands on her bare shoulders, which were surprisingly cool on the warm landing, and looked into her lovely moist eyes. "Darling Clara, lovely Clara! Don't worry! Go away on your trip lightly and easily, and accept this solemn promise from your troublesome little Archie. If I am planning any rapes, murders, or holocausts, dear, I won't do a thing about them until you and Ed are back."

She smiled, pursed her lips and touched his with them. He raised his hands, and they went their separate ways.

TWENTY-FIVE

About an hour later, Archibald appeared, shaved, washed, and slicked—looking much as he had at the Contis' party—in the kitchen, where Edward had almost finished peeling the potatoes and Clara was beginning to cut them.

"We're going to have genuine french fries tonight, boys. None of your soggy frozen ones. I got out the old deep-fry pan—or pot. Mother always called it a pan, but it looks more like a pot to me. You have to fry them twice. It's better that way, even if it's a little more trouble. So you see, I do know what I'm doing in the kitchen."

"And it's after six-thirty and no one has started drinks yet," said Archibald.

"Why, so we haven't," said Edward.

"So may I make a suggestion: that we skip the bourbon for a change and have that bottle of red wine instead, that's been in the icebox for a couple of months now?"

"Well, I don't know," said Clara, looking at Edward.

"It's alright by me."

Edward smiled and let the last clumsily peeled potato tumble into the pot. "The question now before the assembly is: Can one Edward Bromley, Jr., known to be bibulous in the extreme, get through an evening without his customary bourbon and water? My dear ones, after all these years, I'm afraid I have to say you don't really know me very well. You see that pipe there on the sideboard? You've noticed, I'm sure, that some evenings I smoke it, and some I don't. I take it or leave it, as they say, and at any particular time it doesn't make a particle of difference to me whether I have taken it or left it. That's very unusual. You realize that. You remember when Arch smoked, before he went through the terrible and heroic ordeal of giving it up. If he wanted a cigarette and he had none, there was fury, agony, and the climbing of walls. All this poses a question, and the answer, dears, is that your Edward simply does not become addicted to things. He moves sedately through life, mixing without anxiety and without self-consciousness with all that chooses to mix with him and, *ipso facto*, clinging to nothing. I may have been a little drunk—and sometimes a little more than a little drunk—every night for the past fourteen years, but you will have noticed, and you shall be my witnesses, that rarely has my shirt so much as come unbuttoned. If I never saw another drop of bourbon in my mortal life (I shall never be persuaded that I shan't drink it in Heaven), I would feel a touch of generous sorrow, perhaps—but pain?—the actual pain of want? Never. So let's have the wine."

Archibald clapped his hands in applause. "When you die, brother, there shall pass a glory from the earth. A last remnant of a vanished world."

"I only hope," said Edward, placing his hands in the position of prayer and lifting his eyes to the ceiling, "that when the time comes, I may relinquish life as easily as I relinquished tonight's bourbon."

"Don't be taken in by him, Archie," said Clara with a smile. "When you scratch that suave exterior, you get into chaos pretty quickly. You ought to look in his room sometime. It's like those suits he wears: all unbelievably neat. Not a pin out of place. Then look into one of his bureau drawers or into his closet. You won't believe it. Chaos. Everything stuffed, bulging with crumpled chaos."

"Ah, so, the salamander will out!" said Archibald. "Hey, that's good!" said Edward. "That's poetry. The salamander will out!"

He looked at Clara, and then all looked at each other and laughed. Incredible! Archibald thought. In all the years before now, they had never talked about each other's rooms in front of him—not, at least, that he could remember. It was as if they knew he had been there, or suspected. Clara's tale about the stranger was surely her way of saying hysterically that she suspected. Which was not to say that they *consciously* suspected anything at all. They seemed rather only to have a vague feeling that he had become somehow dangerous, more dangerous in a way they could not understand, than he had ever been before; and so they tried to be friendly, to propitiate, to draw him into intimacy with them to a degree that they never had. And it was downright bizarre: in this new intimacy and in their laughter, they seemed to be referring to their incest openly. What did *they* mean by 'the salamander' that 'will out?' Edward's salamander-colored undershorts? Or—in a more conventional symbolism—his penis? Or nothing at all?

Maybe if he simply asked whether they had had or were having sex together, they would freely tell him. No, he mustn't risk it. If they took offense, they would be totally and completely on their guard.

What struck him as really strange in all this was how his suspicion and their new fear of him were actually drawing the three of them closer and making their common life warmer and more friendly. It was like the flaring of the leaves in autumn into brilliant color before they die. Or like a star collapsing into itself, drawing all its substance into closer, deeper intimacy before it explodes as a supernova.

They deep-fried the potatoes and broiled the steak and made the salad and cooked the string beans, all working happily together, and put it all on the tea wagon and wheeled it into the dining room, where they set out places and ate it, talking about nothing in particular: how good it tasted, the bouquet of the wine, whether the salad dressing that Edward had concocted ought to be called French or Russian or Outer Mongolian.

When they had finished the main course and were having the last of the wine with fruit and cheese, Archibald said, looking at the opposite wall:

"Before dinner I was up in the attic." He heard the knife that Clara had been using to cut a piece of cheese clatter on her plate and looked up. They both had their eyes very soberly on him. "Sorry if I said that too abruptly or phrased it ambiguously—as though I were the strange man, Clara, that Ed told me you were afraid might be in the attic—as though I had been up there for a couple of days and finally decided to come down, have a shower and eat a little something. Ed said you were quite upset and made him promise not to go up and look, but I hadn't made any promises, so I was free to go. There's no one there." He smiled. "You don't seem very worried about it any more, but I thought you might like to know."

"So that's where you were go..."said Clara, "O dear, I do cause a lot of trouble sometimes with my silly worries and fears. Forgive me, boys. I don't know what gets into me sometimes. And if I don't, then I guess you don't either. It was such a surprise, Archie, so worrisome, your not coming home last night. I guess I thought the world was coming to an end and that made me think there must be a man up there, making it come to an end. Well, it's over now. Clara has her wits again."

Archibald felt a thrill when she started to mention their meeting on the second floor landing and then stopped herself, evidently not wishing Edward to know about it. So now, he thought, Clara and I have intimacies that Edward doesn't share! And then he thought: Or has she only put it on? She had time, after all, to think it out while I was talking, and then to playact it, pretend to stop herself like that, as part of her new program of making her dear little Archie feel at home and secure. Then, when they were in bed together tonight, they would laugh about it and giggle, while he...I must, thought Archibald, I absolutely must make certain beyond any possibility of doubt that they *are* in bed together every night.

"I forgot to mention," he said, "I'm going to be out for the day tomorrow and probably won't be back until the evening. So don't wait up, if it comes to that. I promise, I solemnly promise that I'll sleep here tomorrow night, so that I'll be on hand Saturday morning when you take off to the Cape."

"O!" Clara gave the little cry with which she was accustomed to indicate that an unexpected pain had been inflicted.

"I seem to be dropping bombshells tonight," said Archibald. "Forgive me. I don't mean to. George Kaskin asked me out for the day on his yacht."

"His yacht!" they said in perfect unison.

"He may be a little ironic when he calls it that. I don't think it's very big."

"But he's a Communist, you said," said Clara.

"Right, Arch, and you know Communists aren't supposed to have yachts. It's like a mouse using kitty-litter."

There was a pause.

"I don't want to go to the Cape," said Clara suddenly.

"Clara!" This time 'the boys' spoke in unison. Archibald continued, "But it's all settled. The place is rented. I know you want to go, so don't make me feel guilty about going out with my friend."

Her eyes flashed. "Your friend? How can he be your friend? He's a maniac. There's something evil about him. I can feel it. I can feel his evil influence at work, destroying us, pulling us apart, tearing you away from us, Archie. You haven't said a thing to us about that party of his that you went to, or the poetry reading, or what you were doing all last night."

"You haven't asked."

"Don't answer like that! Please! I was afraid to ask!"

"You needn't have been. It was a perfectly ordinary evening. I met a girl, and she put my hand under her dress, and I didn't like that very much, so then I met another girl, and she was very nice, so I asked her to marry me, but she couldn't marry me because she had seventeen million dollars."

"Don't do this to me! I can't stand it!" she almost screamed.

"Clara, my dear...." said Edward.

"No, don't touch me!" Her face was awash with tears to an extent that Archibald did not realize was still possible with her. "He's a monster, and I think I've had about all of him I can stand. I wish he had never come home. Why didn't he stay away for good? Why can't he leave us in peace? Why does he always have to pick, pick, pick into everything? Why can't he just get a job and go to work and live like a normal decent human being?"

Her outburst would be over soon, Archibald could tell, and she would forget; but despair invaded him nevertheless. He felt dizzy, and her sobbing seemed to recede to a great distance. Sleep, drawn on by the dinner and the wine, was at last beginning to overwhelm him. He struggled to his feet, and as he was leaving the room, Clara's voice seemed to come near again, saying quietly now, but clearly and distinctly, so that he could hear:

"Dad built this house so that we could be happy in it. Why can't we be happy in it?"

TWENTY-SIX

The next day was Friday, Edward's and Clara's last day of work before they went on their vacation, and no sooner were they in their cars and out of the driveway, than Archibald also, having had a pleasant breakfast with them, got into his orange Volkswagen and, making sure that the fresh-cut key was in his pocket, started the engine and headed for the Cape.

He stopped at the family bank and withdrew $500 from his personal account, made some small purchases in a grocery and a liquor store, and after that it was an hour's drive through the city on various expressways and then southward. It seemed strange to go into the city first, thickening the congestion. He joined a stream of cars that flowed on stilts, like an aqueduct, around the roots of huge buildings, whose use and purpose were an almost total mystery to him, and entered a vast interchange where various directions mixed and sorted themselves into new directions. He and his car looped and swerved, following the "south" signs, until the road straightened again and swarmed through a helter-skelter of sooty buildings and smokestacks, a drawbridge, black and rusty, connecting nothing with nothing, a herd of railway cars with broken windows: a world of doomed projects and giant carcasses to be fought over by wealthy developers and hungry politicians. The city perpetually renewing itself....

Then the slow release: first department store warehouses, lumber yards, and petroleum tanks. Then patches of green. Polluted wetlands. A glimpse of a marina crowded with little sail and motorboats, looking forlorn in their greasy inlet. Then another small interchange, and all this began to resolve into trees and green on both sides of the road and on the island in the middle, growing broader between the two sides, pressing them apart into two separate roads as the miles unwound, peculiar half-roads, each going in only one direction: two strands held together by being opposite to one another, positive and negative, mirror images, like strands of DNA.

Then the air changed, and there was a coolness and a hint of salt from the sea; and the trees along the side of the road began to grow gnarled and stunted as their soil became sandy, and on the right there was a reach of stagnant water trapped by the road's embankment where the trees had died, their branches fallen, and their trunks, gray and splintered, suggested a battlefield.

At last over the green land ahead, the silvery superstructure of a bridge appeared in the sunny afternoon, hovered like an inconsequential dream, and grew to enormous size. He approached and steered into it, and as the car climbed its gradual incline, he could see water far below and sleek sailing yachts with their sails furled, moving beneath it on their auxiliary engines.

Sand was everywhere now. It was a world built on sand and of the stunted things that grow in sand. When he judged that he was near his destination, he stopped by a huge green water tank and peed on a bush. There was a lake below, from which the vegetation stretched ten miles or so to the silver line of ocean beyond.

Following the signs to Annisville, he turned off the main highway, went past a vast new shopping mall with brown mansard roofs, a municipal airport with private jets climbing in and out, innumerable motels, gas stations, and restaurants. Then after a crucial traffic circle, all this changed to paint stores, hardware stores, rug and furniture stores, and funky little cottages that announced that they dealt in real estate.

Finally the narrow street opened into the plenitude of the Annisville docks, and he knew from Edward's and Clara's description and from the address that he was very near their cottage. He pulled into the Harbor Vista Motel, booked a room for the next week, and started out on foot.

The docks were for fishing boats, tourist and in earnest, sightseeing boats, great passenger boats to the Islands, and private sailboats and motor yachts that had risked the passage up a channel well-known for its tortuousness. A long rank of hulls and lead-covered piles separated the oily water of the inner bay on one side from a forest of parking meters planted in macadam on the other. He surveyed the area from the relatively high ground of the Motel parking area on the other side of the street. It was a festive scene with gaily colored cars and people moving everywhere. He felt transformed, watching it. Why didn't he take little trips like this more often, opening himself to the variety and pleasure of life, instead of staying home day after day, letting his pants fall down, mowing the lawn and digging up dandelions? Did he need revenge in order to live?

He followed the sidewalk parallel to the docks toward the beaches and away from the town, and in less than two hundred yards, already among private houses, came upon the correct number, 97, whitewashed on a branch over a gravel driveway. Behind this was a neat white cottage of one story set back more than a hundred feet from the road. The sidewalk was full of people going to and from the public beach less than a half-mile down the road, and he aroused no suspicion as he passed back and forth, looking in at the cottage.

There was an immaculately polished beige car of a large American make parked on the lawn in front, and on his third pass before the driveway, his heart leapt. A couple had appeared at the front door. He slowed his pace even more, doubled back immediately and saw them get into the car, which came to life, crawled cautiously out the driveway, and inched past him into the street. For an instant his look met the heavily-lidded eyes of the man, fat and balding, and with a lumpy nose peeling from too much sunlight, at the wheel.

He walked up the driveway with, he hoped, just the right mixture of casualness and purpose to blend in with the general atmosphere, which he had been observing and feeling all the while, took out the freshcut key, unlocked the front door, and entered the cottage. He closed the door behind him, which locked itself again, and stood in a combination sitting room and dining room on the right side of the building. To the left were a bathroom and a kitchen and to the rear two bedrooms. He looked into them. In the one on the left an unmade double bed with pieces of clothing lying about. What slobs people are, he thought: their car all slicked and aglitter, but this is their actual life. He looked into the other bedroom. Two single beds. One unmade. More articles of clothing.

Back in the sitting room, he noticed a set of golf clubs in a dirty canvas bag and another door. To the cellar most likely. He drew back a flimsy bolt, fumbled upon a string in the darkness, pulled on the light, and stepped squeaking down a set of narrow stairs. He stood on the cement floor, waiting for his eyes to adjust to the dim light. A full cellar under the whole house, he judged. The usual musty smell of cellars. A touch of open cesspool? He couldn't be sure. It was extremely damp. The cold water pipes, that he had to stoop to pass under, were heavily beaded with condensation. He'd better wear a sweater.... There was a red gasoline lawnmower, a table, some old tires against one wall and several chairs, evidently left over from above. He tried one. Comfortable enough. He'd better bring food and water. And an old milk bottle: yes, there was a drain in one corner.

He had mounted the stairs and had his hand on the handle of the open door out into the room when he heard a key in the front door. He must decide what to do instantly. If it was the man with the peeling nose, he had obviously only come back for something, and Archibald could wait him out in the cellar. But what if it were someone new? There might be—probably were—three occupants: two in the double bed, one in the single. If that, then he might be caught in the cellar indefinitely. He sprang into the room and behind the front door, just as it opened.

For the second time in less than ten minutes, his eyes met those of the man with the peeling nose. Their heavy lids vanished as they opened wide in terror and indignation.

"What the...." The voice was oddly squeaky, coming from such a corpulent man, bulging in his tee shirt.

"Excuse the intrusion, old boy," said Archibald in his best English accent, "I'm the previous tenant and I left something behind." While saying this, he pushed past the man out the front door and strode quickly but deliberately over the vast distance to the street.

"Hey, stop!" called the man's high-pitched voice. Good, thought Archibald, he's not yelling, "Stop, thief!"

or "Stop, murderer!" He doesn't really want me to stop at all— doesn't want any help to stop me anyway.

As he passed the beige car, he saw vaguely behind the tinted glass of the windshield the face of a woman. Her mouth opened silently, as though she were a fish in a tank. He could just barely hear her scream, so totally muffled was it by the car's closed windows. The car's probably airconditioned, he thought. Overelaborate, wretched American cars.

At last he reached the crowded sidewalk. He turned right, away from the docks, and kept going. He wouldn't return to the motel until he was absolutely certain he had been lost in the swarm and not been followed. His heart was thumping violently. He felt as though he could walk for miles.

He came to an extensive grove of small pine trees on his left, then, a little further on, to a road in among them and in the middle of this road a kind of large wooden box with a man sitting in it. This must be the entrance to the beach that Clara and Edward had described. He knew, also from their description, that he could enter on foot, but he wanted to avoid as absolutely and completely as possible coming to anyone's attention, so he backtracked to a footpath he had noticed under the fence and in among the trees.

He passed picnic tables where large families from Mediterranean countries were having elaborate cookouts among the trees and came out on high ground overlooking a beach and a mooring area for small boats. He sat on the sparse grass. What had gone wrong? Had he lost his touch, his inspiration, his luck? There was such a thing as luck. He was sure of it. Some people had it, some didn't, and some had it and then lost it. That's all Napoleon wanted to know about his generals: whether or not they were lucky.

Well, but maybe he was still the old Archibald after all, he thought as he walked back to his motel, taking a long way around to avoid the cottage. He'd brazened it out quite brilliantly with old Peeling Nose, hadn't he? He knew the risks when he entered the cottage, and P. N. and his squeaky voice and his wife would be out of the picture as well as out of the cottage by tomorrow. Nothing was lost.

He left some things in his room that might prove useful, some books, a change of clothes, a loaf of his favorite bread, salami and cheese that he had bought in Sweethill, locked the door and drove off in search of a garage where he could leave his car in days to come and be sure that passers-by would not see it. Then he drove to a beach in a neighboring town, snacked on more of the groceries he had bought, lolled in the sunlight all afternoon to make himself feel that he might have spent lazy hours on Kaskin's boat, and drove back to Sweethill in the early evening.

TWENTY-SEVEN

The next morning was all bustle and anxiety as Edward and Clara fussed, dithered, showed a sign or two of hysteria, but finally got into Clara's Cadillac and started the engine. Archibald had both hands on the front door as he bent down and looked into the window at Clara and across her to where Edward was driving, and the last thing he said as the car began to move was,

"Be sure you stop at a booth and phone me as soon as you get to Annisville. I won't stir from the phone until I hear."

"You're a dear to show such concern," said Clara. "We'll be sure not to forget." And the car crackled out the driveway and lost itself among the trees.

Archibald went into the house, found a wide-necked milk bottle and an old attaché case that he had used at one time, and put the bottle into the case and the case into his car. Then he thought a moment, went back into the house and came out with an old beige sweater, which he flung through the car window onto the front seat next to the attaché case.

About an hour and a half later the phone rang. "Edward!"

"Yes, of course, you knew it would be me. Well, here we are in Annisville, Anna's Villa, what you will. Ville, will, well, whatever. Clara has had time to ruffle her feathers and settle into the new nest, and new joys will no doubt presently be hatching."

Archibald smiled broadly into the telephone. "Good, to hear you, Ed. How's the weather?"

"Balmy and beautiful. We'll be off to the beach in moments. Clara says the stove is primitive and the fridge has no freezer, so we'll be eating out a good deal probably."

"Good! You indulge yourselves! Tonight?"

"O yes, tonight for sure. Can I have my bourbon tonight?"

"May Ganymede himself pour you a cup!"

"Good. After the third cup, I'll start looking for him. Good bye, Arch."

"Good bye, Ed."

Wonderful Ed, beautiful Clara! And he asked himself for perhaps the thousandth time why he was planning to do such things to the only two people in the world for whom he felt a love that was indestructible.

> O then at last relent: is there no place
> Left for Repentance, none for Pardon left?

Where had he heard those lines? Edward must have bellowed them forth some evening in his cups. Shakespeare or Milton or somebody. Strange how lines came out of the past like that without his ever having tried to learn them. The process seemed to depend on his remaining ignorant of where they came from.

But why couldn't he relent and submit to Edward and Clara and their benign order? Submit! The question answered itself.

Then, if it was as simple as that, what did their guilt or innocence have to do with it? Didn't the Pharaohs of Egypt live in incest? Ah, but the Pharaohs of Egypt weren't men. They were gods....

Exactly! Edward and Clara had raised themselves above ordinary humanity, above him, Archibald. That was what he could never submit to, never accept. The exalted ones. The manipulators. They must be pulled down and their tawdry painted backdrop of reality crumpled and pushed aside. It was not a matter of whether or not it would please him to do this. It was only a matter of doing what had to be done. Hillary and Norkey didn't climb Mt. Everest because it was a pleasure to do so, but because it was there to be climbed.

He directed his little salamander car southward over the same route as yesterday while these thoughts tossed and turned sleeplessly in his brain and from time to time he soothed himself in self irony with another quotation—

> Ay me, they little know
> How dearly I abide this plan I've made,
> Under what torments inwardly I groan.

He drove directly to the garage that had agreed to keep his precious Volkswagen out of the rain and sunlight, put the sweater in the case alongside the milk bottle, and proceeded with them to his motel on foot. It wasn't far, but he would have to exercise extreme caution nevertheless, scanning all creatures on foot for the familiar figures of Edward and Clara in the distance, and all traffic for a shiny green Cadillac, so that he could dodge quickly into an alley or dark doorway.

When he reached his room, he made himself a cheese and lettuce sandwich, poured a little wine into the glass from the bathroom and, when he had consumed these, he brushed his teeth and settled down with a book from the Sweethill library on someone's new theory that the Dinosaurs were warm-blooded creatures.

He read, checking his watch from time to time, for about three and a half hours, or until it was past Edward's and Clara's usual dinner time. Then he carefully packed the attaché case with all that he would be needing, using his trouser and shirt pockets for some little items that wouldn't fit, and set off for the cottage. The green Cadillac was not there, and he let himself in with his key. He found himself in the same sitting-dining room as yesterday, but it seemed uncannily familiar now. He apprehended the effect without at first realizing the cause. In place of a welter of unfamiliar objects, evidently the property of Peeling Nose and his spouse, which had vanished along with them, there was now a spare, chaste sprinkling of totally familiar items: a bottle of the Bromley brand of bourbon, Clara's sunglasses, the white and green silk kerchief she had worn over her hair when they set out in the morning, Edward's pipe, tobacco pouch, and butane pipe lighter; and on the dining table a box of Clara's favorite cookies. He looked in the kitchen:

their food parcels unopened; in the bathroom: familiar-looking towels; on the washline out the side window: their bathing suits, which he had only seen rarely when they went to the Sweethill pool on the very hottest of summer days. Her suitcases were opened in the bedroom with the double bed; his were closed in the other. How did Edward get out of his street clothes, into his bathing suit, and back into his street clothes again without opening his suitcase?

Archibald shook his head with a smile and opened the cellar door. He paused in consternation. He had to draw that silly little five-and-ten-cent store bolt to get the door open, and there was no way to shove it back in place when he had closed the door behind him and gone down into the darkness. Clara with her uncanny awareness of exactly how things had been left, in all likelihood would notice and reach the conclusion that the strange man was back. We couldn't have that, Archibald thought. We wanted her relaxed, in the mood for pleasure, and behaving in her natural spontaneous fashion.

He looked around helplessly. There must be a way. In a kind of groping daze, he wandered about and into Clara's bedroom. His eyes moved among her things, already quite thoroughly scattered about, and fell on her sewing kit. He didn't know she had a sewing kit, didn't even know she sewed. He'd always done his own mending, up to a point, using a few skills in that direction that he had acquired in the army, and when that point was passed, simply thrown things out. Did Edward do the same?

Or did Clara do his mending? A thought struck: could that be why his undershorts had been in her bed—because she had been mending them? Such a possibility had never occurred to him, so he had not examined them closely when he had them in his hands.

But there was no time now for thoughts like that. All would soon be resolved.

He opened the kit, took a length of white thread, and went back to the cellar door. He put his attaché case on the first step down into the cellar. Then he passed the thread from the cellar side of the door, around the bolt handle on the other side, and back to the cellar side. Holding both ends of the thread taut with one hand, he pulled the door closed by the knob with the other. Then in the darkness (it was dark there at the top of the stairs even with the cellar light on below) he tried to pull the bolt into place with the thread. It stuck. He jiggled the door with the inner doorknob, lifted up the door, pushed it down.... He did not dare pull too hard on the thread for fear of breaking it. Dental floss would have been better. Much stronger. Did Edward or Clara use dental floss? Just as he had resolved to go back and see, the bolt slid into place.

That settled that. Now he was in the cellar for good. To get out now, he would have to damage the doorframe. He let go one end of the thread and pulled on the other to draw all of it through to his side of the door. It snagged. Again he had to be careful. It wouldn't do to have it snap and present the sharp-eyed Clara with a bit of bunched and broken thread on which her imagination could feed when she returned. He drew it back and forth, pulling on the two ends alternately, and finally, a little frayed perhaps, it came through—all of it.

He went down the stairs and settled himself for a long vigil. He was troubled about his performance at the door: his incredible oversight, forgetting about the bolt; his seizing upon the thread before he had given himself the chance to think of the dental floss; his clumsy working of the thread in the dark. Again he wondered whether he was losing his touch. He realized there was something in him that loathed what he was doing, something that had to be watched carefully, lest it get out of control.

He was hungry. It was, after all, his dinnertime too. He seated himself before the table in the most comfortable chair. Best to eat now while he could have the light on and make noises. He laid out the bread, salami, cheese, and a jar which once contained boysenberry jam from Devonshire, England, but now was filled with red wine from California.

Perhaps the wine was not the best idea in the world either; for after he had eaten three salami and cheese sandwiches and drained the jar and relieved himself in the wide-necked milk bottle and turned off the light and sat for a little while in the darkness, he fell sound asleep.

TWENTY-EIGHT

He woke go the sound of voices overhead, male and female, and of shoes, also male and female, clumping and tapping on the floorboards. He was surprised how loud these noises were and how the floorboards squeaked against the joists (probably drawing the nails in and out of the joists) in response to the pressure of feet. The male shoes struck more heavily but were muffled, while the sharp ladylike heels kept up a rapid tattoo. Clara's pumps.

And the voices were clearly Clara's and Edward's, though he couldn't make out what they were saying. Clara's seemed troubled, agitated. Sometimes she seemed to be whispering. Or was she weeping? Most troubling of all were the pauses: sudden and total cessations of all sound, as though they were having a contest of some sort, like children holding their breath or staring at one another to see who would flinch first. The first of these caught Archibald by surprise as he was reaching for the milk bottle, touching about with his fingers where he thought he had left it in the darkness. With the stopping of the sounds above him he too stopped and hung suspended, not daring to betray his presence by so much as a pin or breadcrumb or salami rind falling to the concrete floor—as though he were a puppet, suspended in some magical way from those sounds above. Or rather, they were not the strings that held him exactly, but the motion of the strings, so that when they ceased, he must also, and hang like the piece of limp cloth he was.

What a perfect picture of utter submission to their whim, he thought—Archibald Bromley, the Rag Doll of Silence! He wanted to scream. Wasn't it ironic that in his effort to be free of them, he had transformed himself into this picture of utter dependence? The refusal to submit had brought about the most total submission of all.

This thought made something click in his mind and he remembered now where the lines of poetry came from that he had quoted to himself after the phone call this morning and on the drive here. They were from Edward's lecture on the Devil in Milton's *Paradise Lost*. The thing to remember about Satan, Edward had said, quoting one of his Harvard professors—no doubt a little garbled almost forty years later—was that Satan's rebellion against God was itself part of God's plan. Satan, in rebelling, was, in fact, obeying: by refusing to submit, was submitting. Then who was

Edward to have said all this? Edward, Archibald thought wildly in the darkness, still fumbling for his milk bottle, was God.

"No, Edward!" Clara's loud cry carried clearly through the floorboards.

If that cry had only happened after their footsteps had carried them together in, say, Clara's bedroom, then he, Archibald, would have sprung to his feet, rushed up the cellar stairs, burst through the cellar door and protected her from the monster. But Clara had called from the bedroom a very considerable distance to Edward whose steps had gone close to the door into the cellar.

Had Edward somehow divined his presence below (by balancing a hickory stick on his little finger, perhaps, and seeing that it dipped above the point where Archibald was sitting) and announced to Clara that he was going downstairs to kill his little brother? Or was this all a dream and all this only happening because he had fallen asleep after his wine? But if he was asleep now, he wouldn't *think* he was asleep, now would he? The fact that he thought he might be asleep proved that he was awake. The woman who doesn't drown is a witch and will have to be killed.

"No, Edward! Please! Please don't!"

Years later, Archibald often marveled how the thought had never occurred to him that Edward had simply said, "I'm going to see if there is anyone down there," and Clara had reacted hysterically to the suggestion, as she had in their Sweethill house. But instead he sat, feeling more and more mystified in the darkness.

Then from Clara's bedroom came her voice: whimpering, pleading, coaxing—it was hard to say which. Was this some ritual they went through? In response, there was a low murmur and the great shoes of Edward made their way toward her. En route they paused where the bourbon bottle and the glasses had been, on the table in front of the couch, and there was a clinking of glass as he evidently gathered them up, and when he arrived in Clara's bedroom, another clinking when he set them down—yes—there was a nightstand, Archibald remembered, by the bed.

Edward's shoes struck the floor and, a few minutes later, Clara's; and after that there was no telling who was walking when the floor creaked. But there was very little walking. Only two trips to the bathroom—and even there, somewhat to his embarrassment, Archibald could tell who was who by distinguishing Edward's sedate piddle from Clara's brief gush. He supposed that he could hear these intimate details so well because the sound vibrations were conducted directly from the water in the toilet through the drainpipes to where he was: there were no wooden floorboards to dampen them. And finally, when the toilet was flushed (he noted as a small but fresh piece of incriminating evidence that it was used twice before it was flushed, suggesting an intimacy, a willingness to mix one's substance with that of one's partner), there was a deafening rush of water that seemed to come cascading about his ears.

It was remarkable, he mused in the darkness, how his undertakings—his pranks, his projects—always seemed to get him into positions and situations that were lacking in dignity and had great potential for embarrassment. When he was collecting rubberbands for his rubberbandball, for example, and he bent down in front of the mailboxes by the Sweethill post office to pick up rubberbands from the sidewalk, the other citizens of Sweethill, who had come there with the more ordinary purpose of mailing letters, would look at him with great curiosity. He was in daily fear of meeting people there who knew him, and in his forays into the post office parking lot late at night he may have run the risk of actual arrest. Imagine now, in front of a mailbox, coming back to a standing position, one's eyes gliding up the figure of a woman standing there—the dark shoes on the pavement, the plumpish legs in dark stockings, the dark dress, the full bosom, chin, lips, and finally, with the veil of mourning thrown back from them, the large hazel eyes of Gladys Worthington.

"Hello, Gladys."

"Archie Bromley! You put that rubberband back on the pavement! It's there for children to find, not grown men like you. Now finally, seeing you pick up that rubberband, I understand what you really are. You're completely selfish and don't care about pleasing anybody but your own unhappy, ingrown self. You're not human at all, Archie. You're a monster. Maybe that's what you always were."

He knew that her precise words, when she had found him, crouching in the hedge, watching Nora Melby's dog, Hannibal, would come back to him sometime. He felt sick. Why now?

Upstairs he heard the springs of a bed receive the bodies of Edward and Clara. There was an intimate murmuring and mingling of voices. There was Clara's laughter. Or was she crying? Under the circumstances, it hardly seemed likely. Then presently from Clara there was an indescribably sensuous moaning as the bed squeaked and rocked. It never occurred to Archibald that Clara's moans did not register pleasure, but agony. He seemed grafted to his wooden chair. Roots seemed to be growing from the soles of his feet into the concrete floor, thrusting down through his shoes, cracking, pushing apart the ancient cement.... Those roots, he knew, were to protect him, to prevent him from ascending from his prison like a whirlwind and bursting upon them. Sweat poured from his body in the darkness, mixing with the mildew.

But it was not totally dark. There was a little window to the outside, thickly encrusted with dust and cobweb, which glowed in the dim, yellowish light that found its way into that corner from the Annisville docks. There was a bulkhead door to the outside with dim cracks, and cracks had appeared on all sides between the floor above and the foundation, as though the cottage itself, containing his brother and sister groaning in the sweat and ecstasy of their incestuous passion, had begun to break loose entirely from its earthen foundation and ascend up, up like a pillar of smoke, to the stars.

The desolation overwhelmed him. How terrible, how vile, to be correct in your worst suspicions! How mean and disgusting to be right, to win the argument, to carry the day! How cloying and miserable to get what you want, what you thought you always wanted! How could he loathe them so and at the same time long to rush up the stairs, reveal himself, and join in their pleasures?

There was a loud rapping on the front door. Good God, he thought, someone *was* going to interrupt them!

The groaning stopped and there was total silence. Then the rapping on the door began again. The bedsprings stirred. Squeaks crossed the rafters to the front door, the lock snapped and crackled, and the door opened. There were male voices, one of them Edward's, and then several male shoes came into the cottage. More talk. A little cry from Clara in her room. Then a pair of shoes walked to the cellar door, the bolt clicked, light splashed down the stairs, and a rough male voice with an American Irish accent called, "Is there anybody down there? It's the police. Come out with your hands over your head!"

TWENTY-NINE

"Archie!" Clara rushed toward him, where he stood in front of the cellar door with his hands clasped over his head, facing the policeman and the policeman's drawn revolver.

He had answered the policeman's summons by saying simply, "Yes, I'm coming," and slowly mounting the stairs, while the policeman backed into the sitting room. Clara meanwhile had also come into the sitting room. She was dressed in the same skirt and blouse that she must have worn out to dinner, though she had bare legs and feet. Archibald marveled at how quickly she had gotten dressed and, remembering Patrick's virtuosity with her jeans at Jim Balam's party, decided that it must be a special skill that women had in emergencies. He felt her arms around his neck and became totally confused.

When the catastrophe had begun, Archibald had not had any doubt about what to do. When one is trapped and unarmed, one does not say no to a policeman and his revolver. His emotions were irrelevant to what had to be done and so could be ignored. But these female sisterly arms about his neck were another matter. There was now the necessity of responding in a totally different manner, a manner which expressed his feelings, and this was not possible because his feelings were indescribable. He would like to have said that they were nonexistent, or that they were violent, or in total chaos, or in a dream state, or...almost anything would have had some truth. Fortunately the policeman with the revolver (there was another by the front door) relieved the pressure of those arms by saying, "Hey, what is this? You know this guy?" Edward stepped forward, dressed in a long-sleeved shirt open at the collar, the trousers to one of his suits, and stocking feet.

"Yes, officer, he's our brother, our younger brother." Clara had come unwound from Archibald, and the policeman, a tall florid man in his late thirties with gray eyes and thinning fair hair, looked back and forth between her and Edward.

"O.K. Whose brother?"

"Mine, officer," said Edward, grasping the problem in the officer's mind and evidently deciding on the least complicated way out. "My wife is so fond of him that we think of him as *our* brother. He's a little strange, and he plays tricks like this sometimes, but he's really completely harmless."

"Well, like I say," said the officer, putting away his revolver, "we had this complaint from the lady who owns this cottage. The people here yesterday had an intruder, so she asked us to come around this evening and check. But if this is your brother playing some prank, as you say, well, I guess.... He wasn't here yesterday, was he, playing his pranks? Because he fits the description that the lady gave us: dark hair, tall, moderately heavy. Even had the same clothes: plaid shirt, baggy green trousers that look like they're about to fall down."

"No, officer," said Clara, "I know that couldn't have been him, Archie, our brother—I mean, Ed's brother here—because he was with us all day yesterday in Sweethill, where we live."

"Sweethill?"

"North of here, officer," said Edward, "about fifty miles. A suburb."

"How'd he get here?"

"O he has his own car," said Clara, somehow making it sound improbable that someone like Archibald would be responsible enough to have a car. "He must have come in that. It must be around here someplace. It's orange."No one thought to ask Archibald whether he had come in his car and, if so, where he had left it.

"O.K. How'd he get into the cellar, then?"

"I can't imagine," said Edward. "Hang on. There's an outside door to the cellar, I think."

"And you didn't hear him?"

"Well, maybe we had the radio... "

The policeman smiled. "Well, yes, first night on vacation. And little brother, who's not so little but maybe a little strange, comes to eavesdrop."

Archibald wondered how it would be to grasp the policeman by the shirt below the collar the way he had grasped Henry Melby.

"Well, you people seem to know what you're doing," said the policeman, "so I guess it won't do any harm just to let this go and forget about it. But it's one hell of a coincidence, I'll say that. You'll be around if I have to ask any more questions?"

"Here or in Sweethill," said Edward, and gave the address, and the police left.

After the front door had closed and the engine started outside and the blue light of the police car had moved across the window and down the driveway, the three people left in the room stood in silence for what seemed like a very long time.

Finally Clara went up to Archibald, put her arms

around his neck again, and sobbed lightly, almost inaudibly.

"You've had a rough evening, my dear," said Edward. Yes, thought Archibald: being interrupted like that. Then he felt vile for even thinking the thought. Somehow he was unable to get his experience, his awareness just now in the darkness below, to harmonize in any way whatsoever with this, now, above in the light. There seemed to be no way to fit things together at all any more. He had obviously ruined everything.

"I think that the best thing to do now," said Edward, "would be for all three of us to get in our cars and drive back to Sweethill."

"Yes," said Clara, "I loathe this place." Archibald searched his whole psyche for something to say. There was nothing. He had wanted to reply to Edward that they should stay and let him go back, and forget, if possible, that he had been there. But Clara had answered before he spoke: it was not possible. He had made the place loathsome for them. He understood perfectly that this was so.

Then why couldn't he beg them for forgiveness, and maybe even offer to go into analysis, therapy, or whatever people did to get them back into their right minds? He couldn't do that because of what he had learned in the darkness. That didn't fit at all with what was before him now, but he could not for that reason deny its existence. He had experienced it, and that was that. And he couldn't deny its significance either. He couldn't forgive them. He couldn't just say that it was alright for his brother and sister to live the way they did because that fact and the deception, the breach of trust it implied, had come to mean too much.

So without a word he went down into the cellar, gathered his things, and climbed back into the living room. They were still standing there. He went to the front door and opened it, then turned back to them.

"I'm sorry," he said. "I'm sorry I've spoiled your vacation. I wish you would stay here, but I can understand that I've probably spoiled it here for you."

"It's not that," said Clara, "it's...."

"I know. You think I need to be looked after. It's a mistake to think that, Clara. It's always been a mistake. I've never harmed anybody. So please, do what you think is best for yourselves."

He went out the door, pulling it closed behind him, and up the street to his motel. A large single story building on his right thumped and boomed with dance music, and an illuminated sign out in front announced that the place was called, The Bell Buoy. Archibald wondered if that was a nautical pun on *bellboy* .

He opened the door of his room and stood in the doorway, thinking. Then on an impulse, he threw the attaché case onto the bed and turned to the docks.

People were everywhere. It was a pleasant change from the vacant sidewalks of Sweethill, where the automobile was the proper dress in public and the only really legitimate reason for walking was to provide relief for one's dog. As he passed along another side of the Bell Buoy, there was a burst of sound as its front door opened and discharged a group of youths, stunned, into the silence of the night. A blond boy's head was caught in a car's headlights and acquired a golden halo.

Strange, he thought, they never even asked what he was doing in the cellar. They must have known, or suspected. Asking him would have invited his naked accusation. Therefore their silence was a tacit admission of their guilt. But what did any of that matter now?

He came to the boats. Things were quiet. The last great excursion boat to the Islands was secured in its berth, having discharged its load of people, picnic baskets, and bicycles. A little further on, a large white power yacht clinked glasses in the night, flared here and there with the lighting of a cigarette, and cursed in a loud female voice.

All this life, these couples arm in arm, these children on their sprees, beyond him.... He checked out of his room, found his car, and drove back to Sweethill.

THIRTY

Archibald was on his bed, staring at his dark ceiling, when it lit up from headlights outside and the gravel sounded in the driveway. A car door slammed. The front door opened and closed. His heart sank. Edward and Clara were home.

He checked his wristwatch with the pocket flashlight he kept on his night table. He had brought the flashlight with him to the Cape, so that he could check the time with it in the cellar, but he had never done so. Perhaps that was why he used the flashlight now. Almost 1 a.m. Way past their bedtime. They must have dillied and dallied endlessly before setting off. Did they finish their lovemaking? No, impossible. Did they shed tears? Probably, Clara, at least. Did they try to get their rent back? At eleven o'clock at night? Hardly. Any more than he had asked at the motel office for his room rent back for the unused days. He didn't want to talk to them. But beyond that, it eased his feelings to make that minor sacrifice; for a small hurt can sometimes be used to blot out a large one,

as when he had sometimes responded to the pain a dentist was causing by digging his nails into his palms.
They would know he was home by his car in the driveway and by the half-eaten loaf of bread and the half-drunk bottle of wine he had left on the kitchen table. They would have known that if he had left these things behind when he set out for the Cape this morning, the bread would have been in the breadbox and the wine in the refrigerator. Why was he doing all this pointless reasoning?
He heard the refrigerator door below and sometime later, the toilet on the second floor. After the cellar this evening, he was especially glad to be spared all the steps in between. Enough for him to know that they were home—and for them to know by those same sounds that he knew that they were home.
But in fact, no one was home. No one would ever be home here again. He was going to add, not at least until the Bromleys were gone and the house was sold and the new owners labored to obliterate their memory. But he realized that this possible future for the house was also soon to be obliterated.
Soon. After the final sorting out. There was a little more darkness to go through—or to sit through—before the last searing illumination. He swung his legs to the floor and sat on the edge of his bed in the darkness. Everything was silent now. Edward and Clara were probably already in deep sleep. Sorrow would have eased their lapse into oblivion.
He found his sneakers in the dark, laced them on, and went noiselessly down the back stairs, through the back door, and out under the stars. He had a profound sense of release, which he knew would be temporary. He must walk more in the next few days. Walk in the night. It would be safe enough. Gladys

Worthington and her friends were getting old now, old and simple, and went to bed early. Didn't Clara and Edward? For the next week probably, they would be home all day, making the house, which was no longer a home, intolerable. He was sure that after the first week, they too would sense this, if they hadn't already, and return to their jobs. Meanwhile why not make life as easy as they could for one another in the time that remained?

Their house was on the crest of a hill—not the hill for which Sweethill was named, but a minor sour little hillock that crouched, not even wholly independent, at the foot of the main edifice. Edifice? Why of course, Archibald answered himself, a hill may properly be called an edifice. For, according to Clara, God made everything, and therefore hills, like everything else in the world—atom bombs, cancer, incest—did not happen by chance—chance was ruled out of the cosmos altogether—but by Divine Intention. God made the hill. Therefore it was an edifice.

And it was therefore by God's intention also that every direction from their house led downward: down the curves of Clairmont Street in one direction and down the straightness of Clairmont Street in the other— or if one cut through the back yard, down the precipitous incline of Deep Hollow Road in the rear. This was the route that Archibald, deciding that he had perhaps always been fond of rears, now took. It was, after all, the shortest way to the library and, indeed, the shortest way to everything of interest within walking distance—the post office, the town center...everything except Clara's church at the bottom of Clairmont Street. It was curious, Archibald thought, that, now he was going nowhere, he still preferred the shortest way to that new and dubious destination. Did that mean there was hope for him, or that he had already damned himself in his innermost soul?

Why even talk about damnation when he had no belief in it? Because, he answered himself, if he restricted himself to talking about things in which he believed, he would say nothing at all. What about the pavement he was walking on, with his toes wedging forward into the sneakers because of the steepness of the incline? No, not even that. He couldn't even believe in macadam roads. He was prepared at each step—or so it pleased him to imagine—to find nothing there and to tumble into an abyss. Isn't that what had happened in the cellar this evening? Twice it had happened: when Clara moaned and when the door opened and the policeman called.

No, not the pavement, then. Then what about Cynthia? Hadn't he believed—didn't he still believe—in Cynthia? That was different. That was not reality at all, but a passionate dream, a myth, a representation. Yes, he had believed in Cynthia and continued to believe in Cynthia, in the same way that he believed in *Hamlet* or the Theorem of Pythagoras or the square root of minus one. But when reality in the form of a mere seventeen million dollars made its appearance, like a tough little bottle it opened its mouth and swallowed the enormous, beautiful genie in a thrice and left the lovers staring at nothing but the stopper that now held the genie imprisoned.

Get thee to a nunnery!

Actually it was not the seventeen million that parted them, but his fixed purpose. That, and that alone. Each—he in his way and she in hers—had used her millions as an excuse, a substitute for a reality that was less pleasant. He was indeed too old for her, not because his body was getting paunchy and slow, but because his mind had grown rigid—because, to put it as succinctly as possible, he had already died.

And this was why he would not renew contact with Kaskin or seek any other distraction from his obsession. He was too old, too tired. All that humanity, that vagary of character and motive, confused him. He couldn't change now. He would have to stick with the mechanical things, the inventions, the pranks, that he knew best. And if, for reasons he could not fully understand, they no longer seemed to work, no matter. They were his love; and as another of Edward's poets had said and as he, Archibald, had himself already shown, if he couldn't live by his love, then he could die by it.

He had reached Harmony Avenue, the main thoroughfare, that went from Sweethill Center past the post office, the library, the new high school, and eastward into the city. He liked the new mood of quiet despair that he had achieved, and the feeling of utter unconcern for his own ego. Maybe at last at the end, properly chastised by his failures, he would be able to see what he was—what the world was—with some accuracy. But he mustn't entertain that hope. He mustn't entertain any hope any more—not even the hope of not hoping!

Harmony Avenue was very wide and straight, and its two directions were divided by an intermittent island. It was only in these hours of the early morning when it was almost vacant and one could stand at one end and look down more than a mile of its length, illuminated by powerful new arc lights that shed an amber pallor of death everywhere, that one noticed very forcefully that it was not absolutely straight. It zigzagged in two places, dipped, rose, and at the end of the mile, vanished over a low crest. It was as though the earth, the living earth, pushed it out of its strict mathematical shape only in these empty dead hours of the morning.

He could die by his love.... Poor Edward! He would never again badger them with his impromptu recitations and his discourses on Shakespeare and Milton and with his fey distortions of the English language. The convivialities were gone, were impossible now. He could see that. The avenue was empty.

He must go down the avenue, over the crest. There was a golf course beyond, stretching vastly in the moonlight, a golf course and a pond and another smaller pond by the high-school that one passed on the way. It would take—did take—several nights, all the nights that he had.

He went back to bed now, but most afternoons and every night, like the moon hanging pock-marked and orange in the polluted sky, he returned. He walked past privet hedges, trimmed flat on the top, and looked down into the flatness, where the small stems, easy prey for the clippers, had been sheared cleanly and the larger ones were frayed and ragged, for on them the shears had clogged and struggled. It's the stronger, livelier ones that cause the trouble, he muttered.

He sat on the grass in front of the high school at the fall of day and said to himself: Looking out over the pond with only a duck beside you, you feel like the brother to all things. Then why couldn't he be like a brother to his own brother? Across the high school pond the endless roar of traffic on Harmony Avenue seemed to contain a reply, but it was difficult to know what the traffic was saying. Then a burglar alarm suddenly swallowed what was left of the afternoon: the violent retching of some building announcing that it had been broken into. What an obscene way to remind him, he thought, that he didn't care in the slightest whether the building had been broken into or not.

Why, he wondered, had civilization evolved to this constant assault on the nerves? Was that part of its grand design: eventually to drive every man and woman to reprisal and revenge and so go bring about its own collapse? An exquisitely contrived self-destruct mechanism, a natural response to the twentieth century's witless mania for long life and freedom from pain, as though life had no better purpose.

O Lord, he prayed mockingly, protect me from my shallow philosophy!

Herman Pinkney, a neighbor from Clairmont Street, probably a year or two younger than Archibald, went jogging past on the jogging trail that had been worn around the pond. The new national pastime had been a little late, reaching Sweethill, but there it was, there was the trail it had worn, and there was Herman, puffing along the trail, a cog in the great machine. If Archibald turned around, Herman would smile and wave, deeply satisfied with himself, and for that reason, Archibald carefully stared straight ahead, for if there was anything that he absolutely could not bear at that moment, it was to be smiled and waved at by Herman Pinkney.

When the feet faded behind him, he got up and headed for the golf course; and as he slipped into its vastness through a tear in its chain link fence, night had already deepened. He walked across endless dark space while the moon above struggled with the haze. Incredible that there should be so much emptiness and solitude where in every direction city and suburb throbbed. By the time he reached a shadowy tree on a little rise in the ground, where he could sit down and look over the great pond, he felt apprehensive; and when he heard voices not far away in the foliage, young male voices laughing and cursing, he grew frightened. Men, like dogs, had first roved in packs. It was the pack he loathed.... Then he heard the feet of two joggers going around the pond in the dark. How friendly they seemed! And there were lights, warm, glittering and, yes, beautiful, from the shopping mall two miles away across the water; and as he walked homeward along the pond path, a pleasant breeze blowing from the glitter brought the fumes of auto exhaust to his nostrils.

At last he approached home—he could use no other word—crossing the macadamed parking lot of Clara's church where it joined the ascending curves of Clairmont Street. Three or four dark trickles crossed his path, making their way down the inclined pavement, and he stepped gingerly between them. Then after a few more steps, he stopped and looked up, and there, where the trickles had come from, were four or five teenaged boys standing between two parked cars.

"Hey, the man doesn't know piss when he sees it," said a voice from among them. "Pull down your pants, Bromley, and take a crap. You look like you're ready to."

He remembered nothing between their laughter and his hand on the knob of the back door. He had hoped, he now realized, for some definite inspiration to act or, failing that, for a clear inner command to forgive. But he had had enough of walking and waiting, and he knew now that anything clear and definite was out of the question. He was too hopelessly divided.

THIRTY-ONE

During the week following the disaster in Annisville, Archibald saw very little of Edward and Clara. Both sides seemed to find living in the same house easier that way, and after their first week of vacation, as Archibald had predicted, Edward and Clara returned to their jobs. It was heartbreaking, he thought, how easily they could change their hours in their offices: obviously it made little or no difference to their companies whether they were there or not, just as it made little difference to their company payrolls whether they were paid or not. But, he thought again, what right had he to regard their cases as heartbreaking when for twenty-four years he had found his own tolerable?

He slept late after his night-long walks and vigils and put off his breakfast until mid afternoon, so that he did not need to eat again before Clara and Edward went to bed. But on Wednesday around noon, Clara called gently across the back landing to his closed door. Yes, he answered, opening it, he was awake.

She was going to have calves' liver and bacon—one of his favorite dishes—that evening. Would he like to join them?

But the dinner was not a success. All three were embarrassed, wordless—even Edward—and on their guard, and when Archibald went to his room without having dessert, all three were relieved. He was struck by the elaborate negotiation—the intrigue almost—that had become necessary to bring about even this pitiful dinner together. Waiting for opportune moments, contriving special menus, and carefully adjusting the dinner hour had now become necessary parts of a process that before had been taken for granted and automatic. He wondered whether this was how divorces began in more ordinary affluent families.

Yet outwardly during this week the Bromley household presented a picture of unusual domestic harmony and accomplishment. The weather was fine, sunny but with a hint of autumn in the air, and all three were outside every day, Archibald in a new pair of baggy trousers mowing the lawn with the little old mower that went PUTT, PUTT, PUTT, PUTTER, PUTT, Edward, who loved strange headgear, wearing an ancient cork safari hat as he trimmed the vines and hedges, and Clara in a wide floppy straw hat and flowing flowery skirt, weeding the garden and cutting flowers. It made an image of Eden among the shadows of the great trees—the cypresses, copper beeches and maples—and they even spoke to one another from time to time. Toward the end of the week a yellow truck appeared that had an enormous yellow arm on it with two elbows and three segments. In place of a hand, the arm had a kind of goblet that always remained upright, in which a man with a chainsaw stood. The arm lifted the man high into the big dead elm in the southeast corner, and the man and his chainsaw began taking the elm apart. Then as the elm collected on the ground below, another truck came and carried it off to the Sweethill dump. The din of the chainsaw deafened, but none of the Bromleys minded because it was their work being done.

Even as all this was going on, Archibald was making other plans, and when Monday came and he had the house to himself again, he was ready.

When a car has its oil changed, the dirty used oil, called simply *crankcase oil* is left over, and Archibald had often wondered what was done with it. On Monday he found that he could buy a drum of this oil at a very reasonable price, and he arranged for the drum with a spigot attached, together with an empty drum, also with a spigot, to be delivered to the house on Wednesday.

Edward and Clara hardly ever went into the cellar and never on weekdays, but nevertheless Archibald had the drums set up on blocks he had prepared in a small room with a door beyond the furnace in the cellar's darkest corner, where the storm windows were stored in summer and the screens in winter, a room that he was sure neither Edward nor Clara had been in for years. Filling the empty drum would be somewhat laborious, especially in the rather out-of-the-way place Archibald had it put, but he saw no way to avoid this. He didn't care in the slightest what was discovered after the event, but he must be absolutely certain that nothing was suspected before.

So he devoted the rest of Wednesday morning and most of that afternoon to driving his little orange car to an assortment of gas stations, having the tank filled, returning to the cellar bulkhead doors at the rear of the house, where the driveway was beautifully secluded by a stand of cypresses, siphoning the gas repeatedly into an old five gallon can once used for kerosene, and emptying this repeatedly into the empty drum, which by mid afternoon was full.

In the little hardware store in Sweethill Center, one could buy disposable aluminum roasting pans. They were four inches deep and the largest size measured more than two feet long and almost eighteen inches wide. They were quite sturdy and, of course, would contain liquids—as long as excessive heat did not melt them. Archibald had always considered them rather expensive for cooking, but for implementing a holocaust they seemed very reasonable. On Tuesday he had driven all over the city and come back with more than a hundred of them, which he stacked in the room where the drums were set up the following day.

He was mildly surprised at himself for being so careful and economical in these arrangements. What difference would it have made if he had squandered his whole fortune at it—and Clara's and Edward's as well? Of course, in projects like this he had always prided himself on accomplishing a great deal with very little, but he wondered if that explained his behavior fully. Hannibal's bark burst into his consciousness at this point, as if to say, 'Thou shalt reach no more conclusions!' and all he thought was, 'That beast is getting intolerable.'

The next day was Thursday. Why not Thursday? Traditionally the maid's night out. But they had no maid. Everything was automated these days, even death. If the next day had been the thirteenth, he might have waited a day to honor an old superstition and spite his long-decayed father, who had built the house (as the idiom has it, although his profession was cutting into people's brains and he may never have driven a nail in his life) and who always waxed very sententious about old superstitions.

So he spent Thursday's daylight hours between bouts of Hannibal, planning out every action of the coming night with scholarly thoroughness. There must be no slip-ups. But how could there be? This plan, at least, was beautifully simple. The materials were all so basic and commonplace. (That again was an Archibald Bromley hallmark. Even years ago in the Queensbury School, when he had bored into that electric socket in the adjoining apartment of "Little Miss Flouncing Forest," as the English teacher was sometimes called, he had scorned getting a drill for the purpose, but had simply used his screwdriver on the soft woodwork and plaster.)

And there was plenty of time. He had all night, since Edward and Clara went to bed so early; and everything could be in place in little more than an hour probably. Two at the most. He sat on the back terrace in the sunlight that filtered through the high foliage, while a cool breeze touched his cheek and made the sunlight dance on the flagstones. There had been no rain to speak of in weeks, and the earth was getting parched. Mowing the lawn this last time had an air of being a mere formality. Strange how everything seemed to be changing into mere formality, something mechanical. He couldn't bring himself to care greatly about the parched earth or the future crops that might fail.

He felt pleased with himself and with his arrangements. Everything had been worked out except for one matter which would have to be improvised, which he had deliberately left to the inspiration of the moment: his own fate. Every work of art, no matter how considered and classical, needed something left to chance, something improvised, like the cadenzas in Mozart's piano concerti. Something to give it life, whimsicality, and human peculiarity. It was in the selection of this chance element that Archibald believed his project to be unique. In your ordinary run-of-the-mill plot, repeated in one form or another on the TV screen every night, the fate of the plotter is always crucial, the one thing in the plot which is not left to chance. By selecting this very thing as his own point of uncertainty, Archibald established his uniqueness and superiority at one stroke, proceeding in lordly scorn of the small matter that these small minds held sacred: the survival of one's own dirty little self....

Nonsense, he said viciously to himself, he had simply been unable to make up his mind on this point.

Indeed, he felt satisfied with himself and his arrangements—but not because they were different from everyone else's, but because they were the same. He was really just a very ordinary fellow—Mr. Everyman himself. Everyone feels manipulated at one time or another, and sooner or later everyone lashes back. And in the lashing, inevitably one forgets oneself, lashes oneself. That may be the point of the whole vengeful process: to forget oneself. True, not everyone had an incestuous brother and sister, not everyone had trouble keeping his pants up. He knew he was peculiar. He hated confinements of every sort, including tight belts around his waist. In the age of suspenders he would have had no problem. But the age of suspenders was long past. His very peculiarities, he believed, put some things in a newer, clearer light, just as a photographer's filter, held up to some familiar scene, brings out aspects of the scene that were unnoticed before. Gasoline in the basement was there to illuminate something in the human psyche.

He felt satisfied, yes, but terribly sad too, looking up at the leaves high overhead, fringed by the sun's gold, and across the lawn into the emptiness left by the missing elm. In many ways he had found it pleasant here on earth and sometimes profoundly more than pleasant. Age brought a blunting of the senses, something not so pleasant, perhaps; but even in that, there were compensations. The vision grew less sharp, but in the very blurring of irrelevant detail, one saw the overall structure, the masses of things, more clearly. People missed this who rushed to perch spectacles on their noses.

He felt a sudden revulsion. He loathed his arrangements, in the cellar where they were, as always. He loathed his fixed purpose, his hardened hatred, that had gathered him up and seated him down in itself and strapped him in, as in a railway car that had come loose and was careening out of control down the mountain. He could undo the strap now, he was free, but his only choice was to stay in the car or jump to his instant death.

He glanced at his watch. They would be home any minute. Mustn't see them. Not now. He would pay one last visit to the little pond at the highschool and, if possible, sit beside a duck.

THIRTY-TWO

As he walked westward home from the pond and the sky ahead descended into deeper shades of purple, his own mood also deepened and he realized that he longed to see and to touch Clara, and Edward too, one last time. So he looked at his watch and hurried, and when he entered the kitchen from the back door, he heard their voices still in the dining room and went through to them.

"Hello, Archie!"

"Arch..."

He twisted his mouth into a smile, which he knew must look false. "Have a nice dinner?"

"Why yes, spinach and lambchops. You should have had some with us," said Clara.

He wanted to shout, you mean it's not by your preference and to your relief that I no longer eat with you? But he only forced his smile a little harder and said quietly, "I'm glad you're eating well. May I sit down for a moment?"

"Certainly." There was a coldness in Clara's voice that froze his feeling for a moment. But then he realized that she was hurt. Before he had spoken, he had also thought, Aha! Treating yourselves to fresh lambchops, now that I'm out of the way. And his remark about eating well and his own chilly tone had implied that. But he might better have thought that they were *consoling* themselves with fresh lambchops, now that he was gone or, better yet, that she had been trying to entice him back with the smell of fresh lambchops cooking. For it probably came as a surprise to them to learn by the sound of the back door just now that he was not in his room.

So a look of genuine kindness came into his face when he took his old seat at the table and leaned forward, looking from one to the other, and moving his hands forward awkwardly, one toward Clara, the other toward Edward.

"I've been thinking," he said. "Maybe I ought to go away on a trip for a while. It might relieve things here. Then when I came back, we could start over."

Impossible ever to start over.

It angered him to see them exchange a glance with one another. But he thought of the gasoline in the cellar, and all his tenderness, love, and longing returned.

"Arch..." said Clara, beginning with a tone of pained surprise. But then she seemed to take stock, and she went on in the cold manner she had used before.

"Suit yourself, dear! I think you've always done that, haven't you?"

She was tired. She had had enough of him finally. Him and his games.

"I'm sorry," he said. "I'm not trying to be difficult.

Please, just this once, put your hands in mine...." He pushed his opened palms at them, and looking puzzled, they did as he requested. "...and let me say, just this once, I love you, love you both. You are the dearest, most beautiful people I know."

He withdrew his hands, stumbled to his feet, took a step or two sideways, and looked down at them.

"Good night, dear brother and sister! Good night!"

Then he went to his room.

He waited there while they put their dishes in the dishwasher and went to their part of the house. Then he put on a dark shirt, tiptoed out the back door, and stationed himself on the front lawn in the shade of a bush within view of windows to Clara's bedroom and Edward's. He was glad that Clairmont Street, being in a sleepy, low-crime area, still had the old-style dim streetlights.

Edward's lights went off; then, a moment later, Clara's, so that Edward could get into her large double bed in the dark, as he did every night, no doubt. Archibald checked the time. 10 p.m. exactly, according to his radium dial.

He waited a half hour, then went into the house. Sitting in his usual chair at the kitchen table, he took off his sneakers and socks and went barefoot down the stairs from the kitchen into the cellar. Bare feet were best, he felt, when one needed to be both sure-footed and silent.

The roasting pans would have to be laid out first. He did the cellar quickly, leaving them everywhere there was bare floor to be covered, letting them touch one another but leaving aisles between rows. Then with a two foot high stack of fifty he went carefully up the cellar stairs and, starting in the living room and passing through all the other rooms on the first floor, like a peasant sewing seeds, he flung them casually here and there, letting them float quietly to the floor.

When that was done and when he had opened every door and window on the first floor, as he always did on warm summer nights, and also, tonight, every cellar window, then the really laborious part began. Refilling the old five gallon kerosene can at the drums again and again, he first filled every roasting pan on the first floor with crankcase oil and then every pan in the cellar with gasoline. He thought it best to do the oil first, because the gasoline was so volatile. Once the gasoline was poured out, the merest spark would set the reaction going.

With the incredibly prompt and efficient Sweethill Fire Department only a few blocks—that is, only three minutes—away (he had timed them a couple of years ago, when they answered his call about leaves burning in a neighboring street) he needed an instant inferno that they would be totally unprepared for. A lighted match, thrown into the cellar almost anywhere, would start the flame leaping from pan to pan, so that even if there were no actual explosion from the fumes, the entire cellar would be solid flame in less than a second, and it would burn with a fury limited only by the availability of air through the windows. Within a minute at the most, he felt sure—certainly by the time the firemen could arrive—the first floor would buckle, pouring oil into the flames. Once the slower-burning oil had caught, the temperature would rise far above the firemen's reach, and the fire would be totally out of control. The firemen, unprepared for a petroleum fire, against which water is useless, would be unable to do anything but stand and watch. Archibald wagered with himself that within five minutes the roof would be off. It would all be so quick that Edward and Clara—poor Edward and Clara!—might not even wake up. He hoped they wouldn't.

Doing the oil took a long time, for every five gallons of it had to be brought up the cellar stairs. Last night he divided the volume of a drum by the number of pans to be filled and calculated that a little over a gallon was to go into each pan. Experimenting with water, he found out how deeply each pan would have to be filled. It was a great help to have done this, for now very few pans had to be visited more than once. He was surprised at himself for being so careful not to spill oil on the rugs and floors. Strange how people clung to their old habits, even when the conditions which had called those habits into existence had altered completely....

As he was finishing with the oil, he noticed that the odor from all those pans was getting to be overwhelming. He was thankful for a light breeze coming through the windows to waft it away, but even so, there was some danger that Clara and Edward might be wakened by it. And what about the neighbors? What if someone, like Nora Melby, for example, phoned up to complain about the strange stink coming from the Bromley house?

He checked his watch. 11:15. At least he'd heard the last of Hannibal for the day—and perhaps forever. They never let him out after eleven. But he'd better hurry!

The gasoline went much quicker, now that the cellar stairs were no longer part of the process. As a precaution, he turned off the cellar lights and the lights in the kitchen and blew out the pilot lights in the stove: for all these were sources of possible inadvertent combustion. His eyes adjusted pretty well to the darkness in the cellar, but even so it was pretty tricky

THE INVESTIGATOR

in some places, and he spilt gasoline on himself more than once.

At last, almost overwhelmed by the stench of gasoline, he made his way back up the cellar stairs and into the kitchen's darkness. Always the darkness, he mused, and—good heavens! What if there were no matches? He rushed to the drawer where Clara kept matches. Plenty. He took three packs—irrationally. He only needed a single match. Why supply himself with sixty?

He sat at the table, found his sneakers and laced them back on, not bothering with his socks. Everything was ready for the final flick of the match. Except for one thing. He could do it in two ways. He could toss the match down the cellar stairs and ascend, roasting, to the heavens with his brother and sister. Or he could go outside, throw the match thorough one of the opened cellar windows, and remain unsinged. Which?

He had realized for weeks that this decision posed a moral problem of considerable complexity. At first the answer seemed obvious. Obviously he should expire with Edward and Clara. How would he feel, dragging on in life—how could he endure his own miserable leftover existence, after he had consigned his dear brother and sister to so horrible a death?

But was it right that he should suffer the same punishment as they when he was not even guilty? Consider him and Edward, for example. If he had had the pleasure of Clara's body all these years, as Edward had, then there would be some justice in him perishing with Edward. He was no fellow culprit, however, but the victim, the duped one. He had had only the ghost of Burlingame to sleep with all these years. (At this point the teddy bear he had seen in Edward's room, the large pink and brown teddy bear looking at him with its glassy eyes from Edward's bed, swam into his consciousness, but he could make nothing of it.) And the reasoning was similar with Clara.

And moreover he would not be suffering the same punishment as Edward and Clara, but worse. They were sleeping peacefully now with no anxiety, no fear of the horrible pain to come. For them there might not even be any pain. They might not even wake up. But for him there would be the foreboding, quite possibly more horrible than the thing itself. The coward dies many times before his death, the brave man (and the sleeping man) but once.

It was impossible to think this question out, to reach an ordinary rational conclusion and then act on it. No, for this his whole being must be involved. On this one point, he must insist on being inspired.

Therefore he would sit at the kitchen table and wait. No, he would go outside in the fresh air and wait, and within an hour in the stillness of the night, he was sure the answer would come and he would be able to act with a conviction emanating from his entire being. He checked his watch. 11:50. Plenty of time still. An hour could be spared easily. And no more than half an hour, he felt sure, would be needed.

He rose from his chair and turned toward the back door. But he had not reached it when he froze in horror. Suddenly the soft velvet fabric of the night was brutally torn by something rasping, high-pitched, explosive.

Hannibal's bark.

THIRTY-THREE

Archibald was beside himself. The barking went

on and on, splitting the night into slivers, shattering his nerves like hammerstruck glass, scattering the pieces. Glass! Broken glass! He jumped to the refrigerator and, heedless of the light that would go on with a little lethal spark in the gasoline-soaked atmosphere, pulled the door open. Yes, hamburger for tomorrow's dinner. Yes, well, but they wouldn't be having dinner tomorrow, now would they? He pulled off a chunk and started for the cellar, paused, came back, left the meat on the table, and then went into the cellar.

In a few moments he was back with a jar of glass slivers he had hammered up five or six weeks ago in anticipation of just such a moment, just such an opportunity as this.

He set the jar on the table and began to flatten the meat with his fingers. Then, bethinking himself, he used the jar to push, then to roll the meat flat. He emptied the contents of the jar, glittering faintly in the dim light coming through the window from the street, onto the rough disk of the hamburger, and with both hands (had had to get them greasy with the meat, after all) he lifted up the sides of the disk and pressed it into a ball. That done, he rubbed the excess meat and fat from his fingers with a freshly laundered towel (he was beginning to take advantage of the fact that this was the end of the Bromley world) and launched himself into the night.

He glided over the dark lawn, homing on Hannibal's bark like a missile homing on the glitter of a distant city, and crouched in the bushes where Gladys Worthington had found him, it seemed like eons ago at the beginning of time, though it was only at the beginning of the month. It was she who had launched these events, wasn't it?—her tirade by this bush that had unlocked the whole crazy destiny—he had time to think as he watched Hannibal through the twigs, illuminated by the streetlight, waddling back and forth and stopping at irregular intervals to raise his snout in spasmodic jerks and rip fresh barks from his throat.

There was a light in the Melbys' house. Maybe the front door would open in a moment and they would take him (the dog) in and leave him (the man) in the peace he needed to work out his problems. Maybe he should just wait a little. No, there was no time to wait. He could smell his house from here—or was it only the gasoline he had spilled on his clothes in the cellar? And he already had that hamburgerball in his hand—smaller, less regular, and lighter than his rubberbandball—but this ball was designed not to bounce, but to sink—sink deep into Hannibal's gut. He'd seen Hannibal eat. Hannibal was no gourmet. He did not delicately taste, nibble and savor his food, but down it went with a gulp and toss of his head. No, the weapon was ready and the hand that made it still sticky with it. Mustn't waste good hamburger. O men of brass, you cannot make weapons and not use them!

Archibald's bush was on high ground. This allowed him to see over the Melbys' privet hedge into their front yard. He could lob the hamburgerball from where he was, but it might break open on impact. No, the privet hedge was a good four feet high and would shelter him. Better from there.

He rushed down the incline, across the street, and into a crouch behind the privet's prickles. Hannibal heard him—and probably smelt him too—and his barking raised in pitch and took on a furious panicked rapidity. Archibald could hear nothing else but that tatoo, that bombardment. Horns could have blown, doors could have opened and slammed without his noticing. He had to get out of there quick.

In one motion he lobbed the ball over his head and at the same time brought his head and shoulders above the hedge in order to direct it softly and precisely to Hannibal's feet. When it left his hand on what was evidently a very satisfactory trajectory, he raised his eyes ever so slightly, and there, framed in the open doorway, not four yards from where he stood, was the tall burly figure of Nora Melby.

Their eyes met.

She rushed forward and, in less time than it took for his mouth to open and close, had seized the hamburger, pulled it apart, and felt its contents, and their eyes met again, at a range now of less than two yards.

"Glass! You animal! You disgusting animal! Henry! Call the police! We've caught the sneaky bastard RED-handed."

There was no need to call the police, Archibald reflected. The station was only a half-mile away. They would have heard her easily.

He turned to dash the distance to his house.

Then the inspiration came. The inspiration came that he had been waiting for, praying for in his own odd ways for nearly two weeks now.

He lifted up a leg and, hardly stooping over at all, grasped his ankle with one hand and with the other in one easy motion flicked off the sneaker. He did the same with the other foot and in his bare feet danced lightly into the street. Facing the moon that had just risen, pockmarked and shriveled, in the east, he was surprised to hear his own voice—or perhaps some other voice in his own throat—yip in a remarkably fine imitation of Hannibal's yip. The voice stopped for a moment to allow Archibald to do what he had been inspired to do, namely to turn to his side of the street, pull down his baggy trousers and his underpants, bend over, and point his bare backside at Nora Melby.

Straightening up again, he stepped away from his trousers and took off the dark shirt and the undershirt which, save for his wristwatch, were his last articles of clothing.

"Henry! Have you called the police? He's crazy. He's in the buff." Nora's yell now had a touch of fear in it and she had backed into her doorway.

Then the voice came back into Archibald in all its power and harmony, and it was not a man, but a dog, and not just any dog, but Hannibal himself, yipping and barking in rage at man's inhumanity to man and irritation at the poor fragment of moon, hanging in the tepid sky. And as the voice barked on, ceaselessly, agonizingly, Archibald himself was a white dervish in the night, an infernal vision, prancing and strutting on the dark pavement.

Within minutes the convulsing siren sounded briefly at the foot of the street, and the circling blue lights blinked, falling on the quiet trees and illuminating below them the white car with SWEETHILL POLICE written in an arc on its side.

Sensing the new presence, Archibald gave up his dance and sat down cross-legged in the street while the powerful voice remained in him still. He liked that voice. He realized that he always wanted a voice to speak from within him and for him eloquently and simply like that, a voice that would summarize and epitomize the meaning of things, so that he would no longer need to struggle and plot and devise ingenious inventions to express his feelings.

The car stopped and two men got out, dressed in dark blue trousers and shirts, an older one with white hair showing under his cap and a younger one who was taller and more muscular. The young one strode quickly up behind Archibald and was going to grasp him under his shoulders and lift him up by his armpits, when the older one called out:

"Wait a second, Larry! Hang on! You don't know what you're doing. The first thing to do, always, is to try to communicate with the suspect. You remember that."

"Yeah, I remember that," said Larry, straightening up and hooking a thumb in his belt. "You want to bark at him, then?"

The older man stood in front of Archibald, bending down with his hands on his thighs and said,

"Excuse me, Sir. Excuse me. Could you tell me why you are doing that?"

Archibald went on barking. The man standing over him was an apparition of some kind that didn't interest him particularly.

"Bark at him, Martin! That's what he understands."

"If you don't shut up, smart ass..." He turned back to Archibald. "Sir, we're the police...."

Archibald growled.

"We can't leave you here like this, Sir, exposing yourself. You are in violation of several statutes and we've had a complaint. You understand that we have to do something...."

It was difficult for Martin. He felt that he should address Archibald in a soothing, quiet voice, but he had to shout to make himself heard above Archibald's barking.

"Sir, we have to do something about the noise you are making. People are trying to sleep. People have been complaining, Sir, about your nudity and your noise. Would you like to be wakened by someone— some dog barking when you were trying to sleep?"

Archibald barked furiously.

"Will you shut up, Larry? ...Sir, if you don't stop that, we're going to have to pick you up—this other officer and me are going to have to pick you up and take you down to the station. It would be much better if... Yes, is there something I can do for you, friend?"

There was another man now, standing over Archibald, a tall man in a crimson dressing gown, who had a florid face, a bulbous nose, and a narrow bristly moustache. His large brown eyes glittered under the streetlamp. There were tears in them, and his voice wavered as he spoke.

"My name is Edward Bromley, officer, and I'm this man's brother."

THIRTY-FOUR

"Well, that's good, Sir," said Martin, "Maybe you can help us, then. His brother? Have you been his brother for a long time? ...Larry, I told you! Don't mind him, Sir. He's new to the Force, and he thinks everything is fun and games, and I'm going to write him up if he doesn't shape up. This gentleman here...."

They all looked at Archibald, who was now sitting in perfect silence, staring straight ahead. The voice— the voice of Hannibal—had gone away when that new man came, Edward, his brother. But how could it be Edward? Edward was in Heaven with Clara. Or in Hell. Where *had* he sent them? Asleep on a cloud, a big double cloud with the sheets dragging down from the sky like sunrays spilling over at crazy angles and dragging down to the earth. Then how could this person be Edward? He decided not to worry about it. It didn't matter, because he was never going to speak to anyone else again. He should have thought of that years ago. That solved everything. There were these voices and these people talking now, but it didn't matter. It had nothing to do with him.

"This gentleman here—I'm glad he's quieted down a little—has given me quite a time this evening." said Martin.

"I'm afraid he's gone crazy, officer."

"O Sir," Martin replied, "You don't know. He may have perfectly sound reasons, as far as he's concerned, for behaving this way."

"That's right, like maybe it's just a hot night," said Larry. "Sir, if Martin here sounds a little strange himself, it's because he's been taking courses in criminology himself at Wenzel State for a couple of years now and he's got a different answer from anyone else for everything."

"You don't have to make explanations for me, Larry."

"I was only trying to explain about my brother," said Edward.

"Yes, well, you've got to be careful of stereotypes like 'crazy,' Ed. All the injustice in the world comes down to that. Stereotypes."

"All?"

"All. People's standardized, unreasoned ideas about people. Like 'crazy' and 'cop' and 'criminal.' False ideas, forcing people into molds, turning them into what they're not."

"How can people be turned into what they're not?" said Larry. "If somebody gets turned into something, then what he's turned into is what he is. It's not what he's not."

"The wizard has spoken," said Martin. "You say a man is crazy, so he's crazy because you say so."

"I should have thought," said Edward, "that people *like* to be categorized to some extent. Isn't that how people become intelligible to one another?"

"By telling each other lies about one another?" said Martin scathingly. "That doesn't sound like a very good way for people to become intelligible."

"No, I don't suppose it does," said Edward. "Officer, what are we going to do?"

"Do?"

"About my brother."

"Well, Ed, I'd say that was pretty much up to you, since he's your brother, as you say."

Archibald kept trying to remember what exactly he had done with Edward and Clara. It was silly of him to have misplaced them.

"Maybe you ought to bring him home with you," said Martin.

"I'm afraid that's impossible."

"O, you're from out of town then, Ed? Then I'm afraid..."

"Yeah, he just flew down in his bathrobe," said Larry. "Didn't you see him climbing out of that flying saucer just now?"

"If you don't shut up..." Martin barked.

Maybe he left Edward and Clara in a flying saucer, Archibald thought. A gas-powered flying saucer.

"Sir...Ed..." said Martin quietly. "Why can't you take your brother home with you?"

"Because of the gas—the gasoline."

"The gas-o-line?" said Martin, pronouncing the three syllables distinctly.

"In the basement, yes. In pans. And the oil..."

Yes, it would need oil too, thought Archibald.

Edward sobbed. "I'm sorry, officer. I'm trying to make sense. Forgive me. You see, it's just that this man sitting out in the street like this is my brother..."

Archibald wished that that man would stop using

obscene words.

"...and we can't take him home to my—to our house because he—because someone has tried to—was going to set our house on fire."

"You have evidence...?"

"He's been telling you about pans of gas and oil in the basement, if you'd listen to him," said Larry.

"Just let him speak for himself, will you please? I know what I'm doing."

"Officer, please," said Edward. "Will you try and understand and help? It isn't just my brother. Our house is in danger. My sister is over there in the dark outside the front door. It isn't safe in the house. The least spark. It could go up any minute. I've seen ships go up like that, in the Pacific, years ago, in seconds."

Martin took off his hat to scratch his scalp, revealing under the streetlight a head of perfectly white, smooth-cropped curly hair, a placid, unwrinkled face, and a pair of staring, curiously vacant brown eyes.

"Well, I don't know, Ed. We're not the Fire Department...."

"Please, will you just come over to the house, and then put in a call to the Fire Department, if you think that's what ought to be done?"

They left Larry with Archibald.

"Well, pal," said the policeman, taking off his hat and scratching his sandy hair, "I can't say that I blame you, keeping your mouth shut, or if you can't stand it any longer and have to open it, barking instead of talking. Withholding all comment, as Martin would say. Maybe I'll learn to do like that myself some day."

There's a caterpillar crawling up my neck, thought Archibald. I wish somebody would brush it off or at least put its hat back on.

"That Martin's quite a guy. Martin Hornblower. First

man in the Department to get his degree under the Cultural Enrichment Program. No, wait a second. He got his degree—or was enrolled for it—before they even put in the Program. Lives by himself. Never married. Marches to his own drummer, the Chief says. No love lost between those two. Ol' Martin's right in there with everything new. Jogging around the pond with the rest of them. Stereotypes. O, no, pal, no stereotypes for Martin. That's a real dirty word, stereotypes. Well, I'll tell you one thing, pal. Nobody gives a cold spinster's fuck about what goes on inside of anybody else but himself in this world, and that's one stereotype they'll never change. You don't have to like it, though. That's all I have to say. You don't have to like it."

"What are you mumbling about?" said Martin, emerging from the darkness.

"Just talking to our friend here. I hope that's alright. I hope that's not against the regulations, sergeant, Sir."

"We got to get him covered up. There's a lady present," said Martin, forgetting his theories for the moment. And indeed Clara, in an old bathrobe and with several strands of hair over her face, had appeared with Edward in the far glow of a streetlamp. "Get the blanket from the dog pen in the back seat, while I put in a call to the Fire Department.... Sir, Ed, Mr. and Mrs. Bromley...."

"Officer...."

"Excuse me, Mr. and Miss Bromley. Do you give the Fire Department your permission to enter your house and to remove and dispose of all gas and oil and any other incendiary substances in any manner, with due regard to your property, as they may see fit?"

"Yes, of course, officer. That's what I've been begging you to arrange because I don't dare use my own telephone. If you'd only hurry.... Mrs. Robbins! Thank you for coming out. Excuse me, officer."

The lights had come on in the Robbins' house, next door to the Melbys' (whose lights had gone off shortly after the police arrived) and Elsa Robbins had appeared at the front gate.

I remember her, thought Archibald, oblivious of the blanket that Larry put around his shoulders and tucked into his crotch. She was a ladybug that caught in my windowpane once, and I opened the window and said,

> Ladybug, ladybug, fly away home.
> Your house is on fire and your children all flown,

and out she flew.

"If I can help..." she said, when Edward came over to her. "I talked with your brother at the Contis' party."

"Yes, I remember. I'm deeply obliged," Edward said, although he knew her hardly at all. "Our house is unusable. The officer..." He saw Martin in the squad car, speaking into a microphone. "...is calling the Fire Department. Could we use your telephone? ...Clara, dear. Would you please come over here? Would you go into the house with Mrs. Robbins, with Elsa here, and call Doctor Schmitz...."

As he spoke, Clara crossed the street, staying behind Archibald, out of his sight, and the three stood now by Elsa Robbins' gate.

"You're so much better, so much more collected at times like these," Edward continued. "My mind is such a jumble. I know I'd muff it. My voice...keeps breaking. Would you call Doctor Julian Schmitz either at his home here in Sweethill or, better, at Patterson's

Hospital. See if he's there at the hospital first and have them refer you. You remember Julian. He was at the Contis. We spoke with him, and I've spoken with him since. Tell him it's happened with Archibald. Happened as he said it might. Tell him to send people, hospital people.... No, just don't say anything, dear. Just do it. It's the only way. I've decided. Let me take this burden from you. Let me decide. And you call. You call, please. Because I can't. My voice isn't steady. But you can do it. Tell yourself you're doing it because I told you to."

"Edward..." She looked at Archibald, dimly outlined under the streetlight, and walked briskly into the house with Elsa.

THIRTY-FIVE

"No, I'm afraid your brother hasn't stirred a muscle to our knowledge since we brought him here—what?—five days—five nights ago now."

Edward and Clara sat in the office of Dr. Harold Nesbit in Patterson's Hospital, one of the better known private mental health facilities in the Northeast, which happened to be located within the Sweethill town limits. Sweethill, the pure products of America.... For reasons that Edward and Clara did not fully understand, Dr. Schmitz felt that it would not be appropriate for him to take the case himself and as an eminently satisfactory replacement had recommended Dr. Nesbit, a younger man with a thin face and nervous eyes who spoke with a British accent.

"I'm afraid that's not a good sign. I'm afraid the prognosis is that he might go on for years like that—to his dying day like that. Unless, of course, we jarred him out of it. And then he would go wild again. The dog barking, you know. That sort of thing. Then back to this again, sooner or later—and better sooner than later, I'd say. He's docile—well, no. That means teachable, doesn't it? I'm afraid his learning days are over for the foreseeable future. But he's easy enough to manage. Eats whatever food you put into his mouth. Lets you change his clothes and wash him if you can do it without bending him, that is, changing his position relative to himself. But try to do that. Try to do anything but lift his whole body up at once, lift just his arm or his leg, and you'd never guess from the placid look on his face the power, the tension he's expending to keep himself in that position. You just wouldn't believe it."

"Catatonic schizophrenia I guess it's called," said Edward.

"Well, we don't much like labels like that nowadays," said Dr. Nesbit, "although I must admit they do come in handy sometimes. And in the present instance, your brother does seem to be, as the saying goes, a classic case."

"I'm sure he'd be pleased to know that," Edward mumbled.

"What did you say?"

"Nothing, Doctor. Just a silly thought."

"He'll receive the best care we can give, and we'll do whatever we can, though I wish we could be more hopeful."

"What did we do?" said Edward.

"Do? You?"

"Yes, Clara and I, his sister and I. We lived in the same house with him for twenty-four years, and we knew he wasn't—we knew things weren't right with him for a long time. Since the beginning actually, but more so lately, in the last several weeks especially—something new seems to have started. Clara and I have always tried to be understanding."

"Yes, I'm sure you have."

"What did we do wrong? What might we have done that we didn't do?"

"O my dear man, you mustn't fret about that. You just mustn't. There's nothing that you or your sister, Miss Bromley here, could have done or not done. Theories differ, of course. But it's always seemed to me that things like your brother's illness have a will, a life of their own. Mechanisms, if you will. Nothing anyone can do or say is really going to change anything."

"That sounds terribly fatalistic," said Clara.

"Yes, well, I suppose that means I'm a fatalist, doesn't it?"

"Then any one of us," said Edward, "could have one of these mechanisms, as you put it, inside him, like a time bomb ticking, and no one would be the wiser."

"Precisely."

"Then life is a very precarious business."

"Yes, quite.... You see, your brother isn't really very far removed. He hears every breath you take, so to speak, when you are with him. He hasn't sunk very far. It's just getting him back up that's the problem. We all float somewhat precariously on a sea of madness, if I may be permitted to use that old-fashioned word—some buoyed up by money and success, others by faith, others by drink or drugs or sex, and some few by dreams. Your brother just ran out of buoyancies."

"Could we see him now?" said Clara.

"Yes, of course!" said Nesbit, hopping out of his chair.

They walked down a pleasant corridor with pale wood paneling and little tables here and there with flowers on them. Edward was at Nesbit's side and Clara by Edward's, further off and slightly behind. She had been very silent since Archibald had been taken away.

"If nothing has made any difference," said Edward, "then I suppose nothing we can do is going to make any difference either. But you say there is a remote possibility he will improve, come out of this?"

"Remote."

"If that did happen, what would be the signs of it?"

"Well, a bit of normal human behavior, I should think—as laughter or weeping or a smile or a friendly handshake. That sort of thing. Not something excited and manic. Something quiet and warm. But you mustn't expect it. And now here he is, our Prince Charming himself. I'll be in my office if you need me. Don't hesitate to drop in any time if you have any questions."

"I loathe that man!" Clara whispered as they went in from the corridor.

Do you, dear? Archibald thought as they entered his room, where he sat cross-legged on his bed. Then why do you play with him every night? And such filthy games too. Sipping poontang together, chasing the doxy-posse, tickling the tussy-pussy and tuppery tup-tup. If he could only be sure! And here they were again: King Tutbutter and Queen Nifty-tit, uniting in their persons the kingdoms of upper and lower Egypt, the hills fertilizing the valleys and the valleys groaning in reply. He heard it all in a cellar once. Wasn't he sure? Of course he was. That's why he sent them off on a business trip to Jupiter. Off they went in a gas-powered flying saucer. Gas and oil. But if they went, what are they doing here? If he could only be sure where they went, what they did! How pleasant it was, not to have to reach conclusions any more.

He had relented. That's why he was sitting here relentlessly: because he had relented. Punishment. He was going to send them away, but they didn't go. They were still here. He let them stay. If he could only be sure. But it didn't matter at all: because if he had been right, he had nothing more to say; and if wrong, he would be too ashamed to say anything ever again....

"We had a visitor, Archie," Clara was saying, "Your old friend, George Kaskin. I don't mind him really. Actually he's quite nice. Very concerned about you. He may come and see you, he said. I told him to wait a little until you were settled. He had a friend with him. A Cynthia somebody. The name sounded familiar. Quite a lovely girl in her own strange quiet way. She said she knew you and wished you well. I can't imagine how they knew about it. Do you suppose there was something about it in the paper, Ed?"

"I have no idea, dear. I didn't see anything, and I'm sure Arch didn't. Shall I go on now? Shall I tell Arch the things we agreed we were going to tell him?"

Clara was silent. Both looked at the floor.

"Alright then. Clara and I think we know what's been bothering you, Arch, these past weeks. Well, I suppose it would have been obvious enough to anyone else. We just didn't want to see it. That's the way it is with us. We were afraid. You were upset, Arch, weren't you, because you thought Clara and I loved each other more than—in a way different than a brother and sister should. And we've thought back over some things. We've thought about that evening

on the Cape and why you came down there and hid—
and stayed in the cellar. It was because you wanted
to verify your suspicions, wasn't it? I suppose we
knew that from the beginning and didn't want to think
or talk about it or think about what you might have
heard. You heard Clara and me in the same bedroom
and a lot of weeping and moaning—or whatever it
sounded like to you. Because you see, when we got
back from dinner, we heard you down there—or somebody.
We didn't know it was you, of course. We heard someone
making these noises, and we thought it was some
animal at first, and then we realized... did you know
you snored, Arch? Ridiculous, isn't it? But it didn't
seem at all ridiculous at the time. Clara saw that the
bolt was different—the handle on the bar not pushed
down as she had left it—and that there was a speck
of thread caught on it—the bolt on the door to the
cellar. And then the snoring, or whatever it was, stopped,
and Clara was completely frozen with terror and moaned
and cried in her room and made me stay with her.
What still puzzles me a little, Clara, is why you couldn't
let me go—well, yes, I understand that—but why both
of us couldn't go for the police. She was sure the
intruder was going to pop out any second, and certainly would, if he heard us trying to use the front
door.

"Arch, you were completely wrong in the way you
were thinking. We lived together, helped each other.
She sewed and darned things for me. But Clara and I
have never, Arch, never had anything to do with each
other in the way you were thinking. Clara even said
once jokingly—don't be angry with me, Clara, please,
for repeating this—that if a brother ever tempted her
in that way, it would be you, not me.

"But in another way, Arch, you were completely

right. That's what Clara and I have realized this past week and what we want to tell you now, because you made us realize. Clara and I did, do, and have always loved each other in a way that's strange and, yes, excessive. There are all kinds of arrangements in life, aren't there? Some grow afraid. We were afraid, Clara and I. We only wanted to live with each other in that house, safe, untouched by everything else in life, and we used you. You made it possible for us, Arch. You gave us respectability and helped us to conceal the truth about us from ourselves and everyone else. And we pretended it was you who needed us! That was unfair to you, wasn't it?

"And now that we see, see a little at least, we've been wondering, what can we do? Is there anything we can do to set things right?

"We're thinking of having children come to live with us, Arch. Children who need a home. We're a bit old, but maybe it's not too late to learn. We want to be of some use in the world, not just the selfish people we've been, with our silly pretentious jobs, living—cowering—in that big house that maybe should have gone up in flames, as you wanted, long before you wanted."

Edward looked up. Archibald gave no sign of having heard or understood a word that had been said, except that in one eye water had formed, gathered on the lower edge of the eye, and made its way slowly down, leaving a small wet trail over his cheek.